THE CHRONICLER

JVALANT NALIN SAMPAT

olive turtle

NIYOGI BOOKS

Published by
NIYOGI BOOKS
Block D, Building No. 77,
Okhla Industrial Area, Phase-I,
New Delhi-110 020, INDIA
Tel: 91-11-26816301, 26818960
Email: niyogibooks@gmail.com
Website: www.niyogibooksindia.com

Editor: Arunima Ghosh
Cover design: Misha Oberoi
Inside layout: Shashi Bhushan Prasad

ISBN: 978-93-89136-20-3
Publication: 2019

Printed at: Niyogi Offset Pvt. Ltd., New Delhi, India

To Navya,

For your curly hair, Peppa Pig, and making nespresso with Papa. While dancing.

THE CHRONICLER

Off the western coast of India, 160 nautical miles from Mumbai*

It had been only two months since Captain Nandan Dubey had assumed command of the INS *Shastri*. A Car Nicobar class patrol vessel, it was one of the smallest ships in the Indian Navy, with a displacement of 325 tonnes manned by a crew of 45 sailors and 4 officers. Along with the other vessels of its class, it remained close to the shore to prevent any 26/11 kind of terror attack, and to keep the Indian waters free from piracy along the trade route.

Like all captains, Dubey too wanted the ultimate prize—he wanted command of an aircraft carrier. *Twenty odd decks, not just one. A crew of thousands, not in double digits.* As he sipped some Darjeeling chai, he thought to himself—*15 more years, maybe 20.* His thoughts were interrupted by his second in command, Officer Patil, who barged in saying, 'Captain, we might have a situation.'

Dubey immediately stood up, keeping his chai aside. 'Might? Either we do, or we don't.'

'I am pretty sure that we do have a situation. It's a rather large yacht that's hailing us.'

---

* Earlier known as Bombay.

The senior officer was stumped. 'A yacht? In these waters? Like the ones millionaires use?'

'More like billionaires in this case. It is pretty bloody big, sir.'

Captain Dubey frowned. 'Did they identify themselves? It could be some Russian oligarch and his retinue on their way to Goa. Probably the crew joined in and now the entire bunch is high on cocaine. Hail the coast guard and tell them to help them out.'

Patil shook his head. 'Sir, the captain on the comm said that he would speak only to the captain. He didn't sound Russian.'

Dubey sighed. 'Great. Let me speak to him. Let's go to the comm unit.'

Captain Dubey put on the headphones and grabbed the mic. 'This is Captain Dubey of the INS *Shastri*. Identify yourself. Over.'

The voice at the other end said, 'Are we in Indian territorial waters? Over.'

'Yes, you are. Now identity yourself and your vessel. Over.'

The voice replied, 'I am Captain Aziz from the Pakistani Navy. Over.'

Dubey winked at Patil and sarcastically said, 'The Pakistani Navy is now on board yachts? Turn around and head back, before we take some action that you will regret, Captain Aziz. Over.'

'Negative. This is the yacht of the Prime Minister of Pakistan. Over.'

'I suggest that you take it back to him in one piece. Over.'

Captain Aziz was insistent. 'Captain Dubey. I don't think you understand. The Prime Minister is on board. Along with some cabinet ministers. And the Navy and Air Force chiefs. We seek political asylum in India. Over.'

Dubey dropped his jaw and looked at his junior, Patil. He didn't realize the mic was still on and inadvertently blurted out, 'What the fuck!'

Not knowing what to say, Patil shrugged his shoulders and lifted his hands up and outwards.

Captain Aziz on the comm said, 'Did you just say "what the fuck"? Over.'

Captain Dubey gathered his wits. 'This is most irregular, Captain. We would need to board your vessel to verify your claims. And my men will be armed...' He paused for a second and continued, 'Heavily. Over.'

The voice at the other end was perfectly calm. 'That is totally acceptable. Over.'

Captain Dubey stood on deck as the INS *Shastri* approached the stationary yacht. When they were within shouting distance, a familiar figure appeared on deck of the yacht. 'Captain Dubey, I am Prime Minister Ishtiaq Khan. While your men verify our claims, why don't you join me for a cup of tea?'

Captain Dubey uncharacteristically scratched his head. *I had aced most of my classes at the Naval Institute, prepared for every scenario in the simulation tests. But no simulation prepped us for this! Still, I have to appear to be in control.*

'Sure. Once my men are satisfied and we seize any and all weapons on board, I will join you for a cup of tea.'

The Prime Minister smiled. 'I think you will like it. It's Indian after all.'

Patil tapped his captain on the shoulder and asked, 'Can I Instagram this?'

Ministry of External Affairs, New Delhi, India

Miss Dasgupta was a fairly junior officer in the ministry. Who better to feed to the wolves? She scanned the room and saw a lot of seasoned reporters. She tried maintaining her poise. Momentarily hesitant, her voice quivered a little; she regained her composure promptly, tapped the microphone twice, and addressed the press with a prepared statement—'Members of the press, good evening. Thank you for joining us on such a short notice for the press briefing. Earlier today, the Prime Minister of Pakistan, Mr Ishtiaq Khan, along with some members of his cabinet and his Air Force and Naval chiefs, has applied for political refuge here, in India. We are in the process of assessing the implications and ramifications of granting them political refuge. The reason for their request, as many Indian as well as international news channels have already come to the knowledge of, through various satellite feeds, is that the People's Republic of China has sent in troops and tanks into Pakistan with the tacit approval of the Pakistani Army Chief, General Ahmed. The Government of India would not like to speculate on whether this is a soft coup by the Chief of the Pakistani Army, or if it is a complete takeover of Pakistan by the Chinese forces, until we have clarity on the issue from China itself. We are in touch with the Ambassador of the People's Republic of China here in New Delhi. Thank you for waiting. I am sure you have many queries, but I shall not be taking any questions on this matter right now. Members of the press will be updated when we have more clarity on the matter.'

The press ignored her last statement, and as numerous camerapersons jostled to get a better angle, a whole bunch of questions started pouring in:

'Is China trying to encircle India with their String of Pearls?'

'Why has the Pakistani leadership sought refuge in India, their sworn enemy?'

'Is there fear that the Chinese will invade India next?'

'This is the same leadership which has the blood of thousands of Indians on their hands. How can you let them into India?'

New Delhi, India

Lekha Tandon was having a tough time selecting the saree for today's session. Red would be too socialist, while green would come across as too environmental. She chose a neutral light blue and turned to her lover.

'Honey, is this good enough?'

His reply was instant. 'Anything and everything suits you, as does nothing.'

She found herself blushing at this. They had met at a bar in Gurgaon only a week ago. Things could not have been better. She was finally a judge at the Supreme Court—one of the youngest women (at 41) to occupy that position, and now her personal life was also moving in the right direction. After having devoted her entire life to her career, she seemed to have found *the one*. It didn't matter that he was younger. *Who cares about that these days?*

As Lekha searched for her socks under the bed, she noticed a gift wrapped package. She picked it up, and in surprise, with arched eyebrows, she asked, 'What is this?'

'A gift for you my love, for your first day at the Supreme Court.'

'You shouldn't have.' She removed the gift wrapping to unveil a box marked *Stuart Weitzman*. 'You bought me designer shoes?'

She slipped on the heeled shoes and turned towards Omair, 'How do I look?'

'Taller.'

Lekha smiled and blew a kiss. 'I love them! I shall take you to dinner at whichever place you want tonight—my treat.'

Omair smiled back as he watched Lekha leave the apartment. In a minute, Omair had put on his not-so-fancy Bata shoes—standard issue for his agency personnel, and in a couple of minutes, he was following Tandon down the flight of stairs. He waited in the lobby for her to get into her government-issued new SUV. 'Slick car!' Omair mumbled to himself. Giving himself a bit of a head start, Omair revved the engine of his rented yellow Tata Nexon. He had wanted a less prominent colour, but this was the last car available. It was paid for in cash and rented under the identity of a 'Vikram Patel', an Indian diamond merchant from Antwerp, Belgium, currently on a business trip to Delhi. And that is who she knew him as—'Vikram Patel'.

As he drove towards the Supreme Court, Omair admired how rapidly Delhi had evolved: the fantastic roads, the metro, and the glitzy buildings. The city seemed to be on the cusp of becoming a first world metropolis. Once the enormous structure of the Supreme Court was in sight, Omair found a parking spot and entered a fancy patisserie to grab a croissant and some cappuccino. Wryly he thought, *I have some time to kill myself, and kill I will.*

Three hours later, Lekha received a text message on her iPhone. 'There is another surprise for you, my love. Click open the heel of your left shoe. XX.' *It is a boring case anyway*, Lekha thought to herself.

She quietly removed her left shoe under the table and clicked the heel. A mechanism not unlike a Zippo lighter was set in motion. Tandon and 2 more judges on the bench, and 5 lawyers in the room around her died instantly. 9 more were injured.

Within minutes, the Supreme Court building was swarming with cop cars, ambulances, and medics. A yellow Tata Nexon pulled up at the entrance. Its occupant told the nervous guard, '*Doctor hoon—jaldi jaldi.*' He flashed an ID card. The car, along with an ambulance trailing it, was promptly let in. Omair nodded satisfactorily as the driver of the ambulance honked twice. He revved the engine and exclaimed, 'Allah-hu-Akbar!' The two vehicles loaded with plastic explosives rammed into two different corners of the building.

An hour later, the CNN reporter solemnly stated to a worldwide audience, 'India's historic Supreme Court has been reduced to ashes. The death toll estimates are over 400, including 277 lawyers, judges, common citizens, and an unspecified number of doctors, nurses, firefighters, and support staff, who had reported to the sight after the first diversionary blast. No group has claimed responsibility for the attacks, but a survivor claims she had heard 'Allah-hu-Akbar' uttered by a man who had driven a yellow Tata Nexon into the Supreme Court building.'

Bangalore, India

Vivek Tiwari was running a tad bit late. *But this is Bangalore. You are lucky, if you get anywhere on time*, he said to himself. Tiwari was a recent graduate from IIM, Ahmedabad, and was hoping for a job in his hometown, Kanpur, but when a 26-year-old is offered a high paying job in a hot start-up, one just can't turn it down, even though language would be an issue. He called for a cab and curtly told the driver with an unpronounceable name, 'InfoSoft campus.' On getting a blank stare from the cabbie, Tiwari rolled his eyes and said, 'Formerly known as Kings Tower.' The driver gave him a thumbs-up and started driving.

You either have a death wish, or diplomatic immunity. No one else drives like that, Tiwari thought as he double checked his seat belt. The cabbie had just cut an old lady on a bike, whose mouth was still agape.

The driver noticed his anxiety and flashed him a smile. 'Relax, everyone from Anansamuplampuram drives like this. Trust me, nothing will happen.'

'Where is Anansamup... this place, anyway?'

'It is in Tamil Nadu.'

The cabbie was true to his word and got Tiwari to the InfoSoft campus 20 minutes earlier than scheduled. There was a new Starbucks in the vicinity. They seemed to be mushrooming everywhere. He had more than enough time to grab a quick cappuccino as well. *It is amazing how much of Americana has seeped into Bangalore, a city, which, merely a couple of decades ago, couldn't have been more different. But then, Americana spread around the globe faster than Usain Bolt. Why should India be spared?*

As Tiwari smoked a Marlboro and sipped his coffee, he quickly ran over his presentation on his Microsoft Surface. Towards the end, his thoughts were interrupted by a whirring sound coming from right above him. He looked up. *That flock of birds is moving too fast. Jeez! Those are not birds—they are radio-controlled aircraft. And it's not one flock—there are three or four flocks. There must be 40 or 50 planes.* He shut down the presentation and switched his Surface to video mode.

He watched with horror as one mini plane after another crashed into the InfoSoft establishment. Some hit the walls, while some broke the windows and crashed into the building. There were a series of miniature blasts. *Those things are loaded with plastic explosives!* Soon he could see fumes emanating from some of the windows. Within a minute there was a second wave of attacks. Tiwari heaved a sigh of relief as he could finally hear sirens blaring in the background. Three fire trucks appeared on the horizon. People had begun to evacuate the building—some of those emerging were coughing. *Surely they can't bring down a building with those mini planes, can they?*

As the fire trucks got closer, he noticed something weird. They were green, while they were supposed to be red. He tried pointing out the anomaly to the guard letting the trucks in, but he was too late. One by one, the three trucks slammed themselves into different, and apparently, strategic parts of the building. He smelled fuel. *Those bastards must have filled the fire trucks with explosives.* He felt small chunks of concrete fall on him; he put his tablet into his satchel and made a run for it. He grabbed the guard next to him and pulled him down to the ground. Moments later, he heard a deafening blast and felt a tremendous heat wave wash over him, followed by debris…

Two hours later

A CNN reporter outlined: 'In what was the first major terror attack on Bangalore city, the terrorists have successfully brought down the headquarters of one of India's most prestigious software companies. We do not have confirmation, but the death toll is expected to cross 500. I have with me an onlooker, Mr Vivek Tiwari, who has provided us the first images to emerge from this travesty, which he recorded on his tablet when the first RC aircraft struck the InfoSoft building. You are lucky to be alive, Mr Tiwari. What are you going to do next?'

'Two things: never give up smoking, and write a "Rs 1,00,000" donation cheque to an orphanage in Anansamuplampuram.'

'Where is that?'

'Tamil Nadu,' he deadpanned.

Mumbai, India

Like most buildings in South Mumbai, the Bombay Stock Exchange in the Phiroze JeeJeebhoy Towers too faced a water shortage. This was circumvented in the usual way—tankers filled with water arrived each morning to fill the overhead tanks.

The guard on duty, Vinay Shukla, noticed that a new driver had brought the tanker in. He checked the number plate and duly let him in. Shukla watched disinterestedly as the pump was used to fill the water tank atop the 29-storeyed building. The second tanker too was driven by a new driver and this time, Shukla questioned him. He replied, '*Badli ka hoon.*' Not yet satisfied, Shukla asked for his license. Although irregular, all seemed in order, so Shukla let him in. When there was a third driver who was also new, Shukla realized that something was amiss. He asked the driver to get down and called the cops outside the Stock Exchange. Immediately, the driver tried to run. He was grappled by Shukla and tackled down, but as the cops came running, the third driver laughed and said, 'Our work here is done.' The cop opened the tap of the tanker and said, 'This is not water, this is petrol! How many tankers have gone in already?' Shukla shook his head and held up two fingers. The cops winced—they knew it was too late. Almost immediately, there was a detonation, and debris started falling on the heads of the cops and the guards who instinctively rushed out. They managed to get out of the building and dragged the terrorist out with them, even as he kicked and tried to wrestle free. As they exited the building, the tower began to collapse, while people tried to rush out through various exits. Shukla saw people either gathering and recording videos on their cell phones, or running helter-skelter. Some tried to enter the collapsing structure to help those who got trapped inside, but were restrained from doing so by the first ring of security. A stranger offered the debris-covered cops a bottle of water. In a matter of no time, the oldest stock exchange in Asia had been reduced to rubble.

The seasoned news reporter, Ms Chandra, looked shaken, as she said, 'It seems that today, the economic, political, and software capitals of India were targeted in a coordinated terrorist attack. We have on our panel the former head of India's foreign intelligence agency, the Research & Analysis Wing, commonly known as RAW, Mr Alok Triveni. What next, Mr Triveni?'

Triveni, usually a calm presence even in the mad din of jingoistic news channels, was fuming. 'It is too early to tell. But I can assure you that there will be retaliation and it will be swift and brutal. This new Indian government takes no prisoners.'

Ms Chandra continued, 'We are now joined by Retired General Asim Hussain from the Pakistani Army, live, via Skype, from Rawalpindi. General Hussain, what do you make of this? Do you think it has anything to do with India offering political refuge to your erstwhile leadership?'

General Hussain appeared in a much more sombre mood, dressed in a blazer with a military issue cravat knotted around his neck. 'Let me begin by offering my condolences to the Indian people. However, even before the dust has settled, as usual, the Indian media has started blaming Pakistan. There are multiple separatist movements going on in India; anyone could be responsible. You have Maoists, you have Sikh Khalistanis, you have people in the North East. India has always had some sort of trouble going on with its own citizens. It finds Pakistan a convenient punching bag. We will not be surprised, if the Indian government has staged this attack to give Pakistan a bad name.'

Triveni cut in, 'Is this a joke? A bad name? What sort of reputation does Pakistan enjoy in the world? It is hardly spoken of in the same breath as Norway and Sweden. It has shielded terrorists, it has engaged in nuclear blackmail, as it has engaged in nuclear proliferation. Where was Osama found? The world doesn't need a terror attack on Indian soil to know that Pakistan is nothing but a rogue state, and a state sponsor of terrorism.'

The anchor decided to intervene. 'I understand that emotions are running high. Even I am having a hard time keeping my emotions in check. But I would like to know, Mr Triveni and General Hussain, what do you think will happen next?'

General Hussain replied, 'Absolutely nothing. We are a nuclear state, and if India decides to conduct some military operation on Pakistani soil, we will use all means at our disposal to repel the Indian threat perpetrated by this false flag attack.'

Triveni, with utter disdain writ all over his weathered face, countered, 'Their country is no longer run from Islamabad; it is being run from Beijing. Their entire history is littered with coups and foreign governments controlling puppet regimes.'

General Hussain finally began to get provoked. 'Ridiculous. The Chinese troops are here to protect Pakistani citizens and their interests.'

Triveni taunted, 'Can't the Pakistani Army do that?'

Hussain once again shouted, 'We don't need India telling us what to do.'

Triveni replied, 'The ball is in our court. We have tolerated enough. I reckon that there will be some military action from the Indian side. They can't get away with this every time. The retaliation will be at the time and place of our choice. Rest assured, they will pay.'

Hussain let out a cynical laugh. 'We have been hearing this since eons. We are a nuclear state with Chinese troops on our soil. Do what you can.'

Langley, Virginia, USA

At the CIA Headquarters, heads were already rolling. The Director of CIA had been forced to resign and the Station Chief in Islamabad had been transferred to some backwater posting.

With the proverbial sword hanging over his skull, the Head of the South Asia desk, Andrew McGregor, entered into a video call with the Secretary of State. McGregor thought, *26 years of steady, though unspectacular service, is about to come to an abrupt end.*

No pleasantries were exchanged. There was nothing warm in the air.

The Secretary of State, Robert Upton, said, 'Andy, how are things at Langley?' He spoke with a thick Southern accent, always a problem for Boston boys like McGregor.

McGregor wasn't about to make excuses; he never did. 'Well Mr Secretary, as you can imagine, things are pretty tense. It was a massive intelligence failure.'

The Secretary's face reddened; he was just about done with civility. 'That's a fucking understatement, Andy, and you know it. CIA's budget in Pakistan is more than the budget of the State of Pakistan in Pakistan! We have drones, intelligence officers on the ground, and age-old military relations with their top brass. How, in the name of the Lord, does China plan a military coup in Pakistan and we don't even have a whiff?'

McGregor shuffled in his seat. 'There is no other way to say it, sir. It was a massive failure. We have always had our sights on the Haqqani network, on LeT, on JeM—we really did not bother much with the internal politics of Pakistan. And it has always been chaotic.'

But one matter required urgent attention. The Secretary asked, 'More importantly, Pakistan is the conduit through which our supply routes to Afghanistan run. What's their status?'

McGregor was glad he had a handle on that. 'All supply lines are secure. Before he resigned, the Chief of the Islamabad station met with General Ahmed and the Chinese Ambassador, and got their assurance that our arrangements with Pakistan would be honoured.'

The Secretary slammed his desk. 'For now. Just for now, Andy. We know the Chinese. They will extract their pound of flesh at some point or the other.'

'Sir, yes. I reckon you might be right. Our only alternate route is via Iran through the Indian-managed Chahbahar port. And the Iranians obviously hate us. We can talk to the Indians, if you like. It will buttress their ego and we can come to an arrangement. Indians give us access to the port and the route to Afghanistan, and in exchange, we lift some of the sanctions on Iran.'

Secretary Upton digested that information. 'You do know the current President hates the Iranians. Even if the President comes around, we will have to take into account the domestic fallout, and all that will take a fair bit of time. But we will eventually have to get this done; there's no point relying on the Pakistanis now. Speaking of the Indians, that was another failure. Did we not see any of those attacks coming?'

McGregor shook his head, 'Honestly, sir, there are so many threats in South Asia at any given point of time that it is difficult to filter them out. There was nothing in there that would have given us an indication of the terror strikes. Besides, our network in India is nowhere near as robust as it should be. Since the Cold War days...'

'Get over the damn Cold War already.' The Secretary did not look very happy. 'What will the Indians do?'

McGregor cracked a wry smile. 'They have always been pacifists. But they are pretty desperate to shed that tag. With China in the mix now, there will be a lot of pressure to do something militarily. Their government has been elected on a more muscular narrative. There will be some kind of retaliation, either covert, or overt.'

Secretary Upton said, 'Well, we can't let that happen. They are seen by the Chinese and Pakistanis as our allies. It could jeopardize our supply lines. Rein them in. Give them whatever assistance we can to track the perps of the terror attack and promise them that we will help them however we can. But make sure that no military action takes place.'

McGregor let out a deep breath. 'Easier said than done. I will have to fly to New Delhi. It would make our sincerity seem more robust.'

Secretary Upton said, 'Well then, Andy, get on a plane ASAP. But there is one more thing...'

'Yes, sir?'

The Secretary continued, 'Prime Minister Khan—he has sought refuge in India. Aren't they eternal enemies in the Biblical sense of the phrase?'

McGregor hesitated, as he considered his reply. 'It does make sense, actually.'

The Secretary persisted. 'But how? Even if he would have been hot potato for us, or the Brits, he could still have walked into the Swedish or Norwegian Embassy, and those tree loving liberals would have given him refuge.'

McGregor shook his head. 'In those deck of the woods, diplomatic enclaves are not deterrents. In Afghanistan, former President, Najibullah, was in the UN Compound, when Kabul fell and the Taliban took over. They took him out, castrated him, shot him in the head, and then dragged his and his brother's bodies out onto the streets by tying them behind trucks. They finally hanged their bodies for public and press viewing.'

'Jesus!'

'Yes. So, if Khan saw this as the only exit, I don't blame him.'

Secretary Upton said, 'Well, that explains a lot. Just one more thing. The Deputy Director will be taking over as Director for now. I was not sure whether to fire you, or not; the fact is, you are one of the best hands we have in South Asia. However, another major screw up from that region, and your head will roll.'

McGregor nodded with relief. He had lived to fight another day. 'Understood.'

A week later
MindCorp, Mumbai, India

Trevor Davis was browsing through the Mumbai Expat listings on a social media network. While he had kind of gotten used to it, had even warmed up to India and its idiosyncrasies, once in a while, he just wanted to hang out in a bar with fellow Americans. He could even tolerate the Brits now, who often acted as if they knew more about India, like a former landlord. It had only been a week since the attack and people were reluctant to throng clubs and lounges. But it would eventually pick up. Mumbai seemed to take everything in its stride. It was like a dystopian, post-apocalyptic version of a thriving city in an alternative Mad Max universe. It always moved on, waiting for the next calamity to strike—either natural or man-made. His thoughts were interrupted when a peon opened his door. 'Sir, your appointment is here.'

Davis quickly adjusted his tie and closed the social media tab on his screen.

'Send them in.'

He then checked himself in the full-length mirror and caressed the creases off his suit jacket. He had to look good. He was not a door-to-door salesperson; he was selling a unique and ridiculously expensive product targeted at a very exclusive and wealthy clientele. But the rules were the same—you had to look good. Gimmickry doesn't change, whether you are a door-to-door cosmetics salesperson, or are selling a million-dollar service.

As the couple walked in, Davis instantly recognized them. They were regulars on the Mumbai society columns, old money from South Bombay or 'SoBo' as the local popular parlance went. But Davis did not show a flicker of recognition, feigning the required ignorance.

He introduced himself with a firm handshake. The man had a tight grip, clearly used to negotiations. As the wife shook his hand, Trevor thought, *the woman is obviously more of an air kisser*. 'I am Trevor Davis. Welcome to MindCorp. How can I be of assistance today?' He rang the buzzer and a butler appeared, dressed like he was an extra from the sets of *Downton Abbey*. Davis could hardly keep a straight face each time the butler walked in, but he said to himself, *presentation matters*. The butler set forth a tray with masala chai in front of the clients and offered them a menu. Trevor gestured, 'Please, whatever you like.' Both of them politely refused. The woman then changed her mind and said, 'I wouldn't mind some wasabi peas.' The butler smiled, 'Right away, madam.'

The husband spoke. 'I am Ashish Thakur; this is my wife, Rekha Thakur. We've heard about your services from friends, and obviously, from the media. Mr Bandookwala recommends you highly as well.'

Davis said, 'Yes, I handled Mr Bandookwala's case myself. Well, welcome to MindCorp. I do not wish to bore you with a typical PowerPoint presentation. Tell me what you know about us and we can take it up from there.'

Mr Thakur looked at his wife, who nodded her head. Before he could speak, she did. 'You allow the dead to be living for a while?'

Davis shook his head. 'I am sorry Mrs Thakur, but this is a common misconception. We are scientists, not shamans. The correct way to state it would be that we preserve the memories of the dead.'

'Can you possibly elaborate on that?'

'Of course.' He opened his drawer and pulled out an ancient 1.44 MB floppy. 'This stores memory, 1.44 MB of it. Over the last few decades, we have shrunk the size of the storage device and have dramatically increased its capacity. The human mind is not unlike a hard drive. Of course, it is a lot more complex than your USB stick. Depending on the age and size of the human brain, this complex organ stores anywhere between 1 terabyte to 2 petabytes of data. The variance is quite high—this is a biological phenomenon. We here at MindCorp marry our physics to nature's biology. So it tends to get even more complicated. Are you with me so far?'

The couple nodded their heads in unison, but neither seemed very sure. This was by design. Davis now decided to make it simpler. 'Your brain is like a hard drive. It saves memories. Some memories are real. Some are wishes. Some are sad. Some are happy. Births, weddings, funerals, break-ups—these leave a lasting impression on the human brain. Based on our experience and extensive research, it can be said people tend to vividly remember the good and the bad times in their lives. The birth of a child. The death of a loved one. The first day of a new business. The most important things, like a bank locker number. They may not remember a regular day, but invariably they tend to remember days of importance. Of course, they can forget, but that is very rare.'

Davis paused for effect, then continued, 'At MindCorp, we make a sort of photocopy, or a Xerox copy if you like, of the brain. If you have a good original copy, the photocopy comes out excellent. If not, the photocopy comes out faded. But most memories worth remembering are always well preserved.'

Mr Thakur cut in, 'So if we want, we can just view the memory of that deceased person.'

Davis said, 'Yes, but it is not like watching Netflix, you know. What we need is a conduit, a medium. All memories are stored in our neural network. We have specialists—highly trained personnel, with high IQs, and with brain capacities in excess of 3 petabytes. Such an individual is called a 'Chronicler'. They are plugged into our neural network and they can project the memory of the deceased onto a screen through their minds. Again, there will be some variations—a dress might be of a different colour, or a Coke bottle in a memory could be replaced by a Pepsi bottle. That depends on how the deceased remembers that life event.'

Davis could see now that the couple was hooked. *Time to reel it in.* 'So in a way, you were right, Mrs Thakur. We keep them alive. You can see the world as they saw it. You can almost sense their emotions. Sometimes, they even remember the way a place or person smelled. We are working on a technology which will enable us to replicate that smell, and let it waft through the room in which you are watching. We are calling it the Olfactory Package, which will soon be available for an additional sum.'

Mr Thakur's mouth was agape. 'That sounds impossible.'

Davis shrugged his shoulders, 'Why not? Your sense of smell is also a memory. We can replicate it to a very accurate approximation based on our database.'

Mrs Thakur asked, 'What if there is no memory?'

'It happens. Which is also precisely why we avoid taking subjects who have a history of memory related diseases, like Alzheimer's or Dementia.'

Mr Thakur asked, 'So if there are no diseases, is it an exact image that is projected?'

Davis clarified, 'It is an approximation. Let me give you another example. Maybe the Coke-Pepsi one was too generic.'

'Sure.'

Davis rubbed his palms for theatrical effect. 'Say you have a vivid memory of a hotel you visited five years ago. Maybe you had one drink too many. In your memories, the door to your hotel room was black, when in reality, it was off-white. Based on your memories, we will be able to project a black door and not an off-white one. Our system reads your memories, it doesn't correct them.'

'Yes, that makes sense,' said Mr Thakur. 'So, how do you store these memories?'

Davis's eyes lit up. The clients were hooked. 'If we know that a person is dying, or is recently deceased and the brain is undamaged, then within 6 hours of his or her demise, we bring them into MindCorp. Here we plug their brain into the brain of one of our highly trained Chroniclers, and we back up the memories of the deceased into the neural network.'

'So, we just access the neural network? All the memories are preserved there?'

'Not quite. The neural network stores all the data. Think of it as the *hard drive*. The Chronicler, who is our employee, accesses that data briefly—think of him as the CPU and the memories are then projected on the screen. Artificial Intelligence is not sophisticated enough to store the sheer size of the human brain. Maybe we will get there in 50 years, or maybe 10, or maybe 100.

No one really knows. Right now, the Chronicler is the crucial conduit between the deceased and the neural network.'

'And how do you choose these...Chroniclers?'

'Phew! It is a long process and only a select few make it.' Davis explained, 'First, one has to be extremely intelligent, with a very high IQ. We are talking Mensa level. This is because, they have to briefly store the memories of two people—memories of their own, and also those of the deceased. As mentioned before, the approximate capacity of each Chronicler's brain is about 3 petabytes.'

'And?'

'And they have to be physically in the best possible shape. You see, it is not just the mind that has to be in the top 1 per cent. Even physically, the rest of the body should be able to cope with the brains of two people simultaneously. That's precisely why our Chroniclers are continuously monitored under sedation, when plugged into the network. A little variance and they could haemorrhage. To ensure that they meet our high mental and physical standards, each of the Chroniclers is assigned a personal trainer who keeps them in incredibly good shape.'

'Most importantly, what's the cost?' asked Mr Thakur.

'Well, memories are priceless.' Davis then smiled widely. 'But we are an American company, so we can pretty much put a price on everything.'

'Yes, we have noticed. To be honest, we need it for my father who is in the hospital, and...' Thakur seemed to be at a loss for words; regaining his composure, he completed, '...may not make it.'

Davis was immediately apologetic. He truly didn't like this part of the sales pitch. 'My genuine condolences, Mr Thakur.

I know this is a difficult time for you and your family. The MindCorp process would set you back by $5 million per patient.'

Mr Thakur replied, 'That's quite a significant amount in Indian rupees.'

Davis shrugged his shoulders, while not wanting to appear insensitive. 'It is a significant amount in any currency, Mr Thakur. As I said, memories are priceless. But we can work something out, since you come recommended by an old client.'

'Yes, here is my e-mail address and contact details...' Mr Thakur held his cell phone up. Davis removed his phone and touched it to Thakur's phone. He heard a beep, the data had been transferred. 'Send me a quote and we can take it from there. Thank you for seeing us this late in the evening; his hospitalization was sudden.'

'We run a 24x7 operation, Mr Thakur,' said Davis. 'We understand that we might be needed anytime. I assure you that we will send you a quote within the next 2–3 hours. Is there anything else?'

The peon came rushing in—'Sir, there is an emergency!'

Davis got up and shook hands with the Thakurs warmly, 'Well, duty calls. I am sorry, I wasn't able to offer you more refreshments. Next time, perhaps?' He didn't wait for a reply, as he followed the peon. 'Although, we obviously wish that there is never a next time.'

Davis looked at his Xeric wristwatch: it was close to 11 pm. He could've used a coffee. He approached the gentleman awaiting him. He noticed that the man waiting for him was quite tall for an Indian, at least 6 feet 2 inches. The man had an extremely firm handshake—another fact not unnoticed by Davis. He asked, 'Sir, do you have an appointment?'

The man spoke with a neutral accent, 'No, I don't.'

'Usually, we prefer it, if a prior appointment is taken.'

The man said, 'So you can research the potential net worth of the client seeking your appointment and whether your firm will even bother presenting him with an offer. Else, why waste everyone's time?'

Davis smiled. 'Time is money, sir.'

The man said, 'I know.' He opened his briefcase. It had $5 million in cash. 'And time is not a luxury I have. But do I have your attention now?'

Davis took a deep breath and shut his eyes briefly. He reopened them as he said, 'Undiluted.'

The man replied, 'I need a body processed.'

'When?'

'Now. It is my uncle. He passed away with some extremely important secrets.'

'Usually we need a death certificate, forms from hospitals, permission from family members—there is a lot of paperwork.'

The man replied, 'What is the time window within which the body needs to begin being processed?'

'6 hours, give or take. Anything above 10 hours and it is usually too late,' said Davis.

The man said, 'It has already been 4 hours since his demise. I will give you all the paperwork you need after the process. But if you need an incentive to cut the red tape and the bullshit,' he presented another package from his coat, 'here is $50,000.' He looked out of the window; it was still raining torrentially. He said with a smile, 'Save it for a rainy day.'

Davis pocketed the cash. 'You got yourself a deal, Mr...' he paused for the man to complete the sentence.

'Sinha, you can call me Mr Sinha,' said the man and proceeded to shake Davis's outstretched hand with a smile.

Indoor Gym, MindCorp, Mumbai

The Israeli trainer, Elad, was monitoring Udai, as he completed his third set of tricep curls. Elad looked at his chart. 'You are in as good a shape as ever, Udai. Have you been taking the whey?'

Udai felt a touch of pride. He had been putting in some serious effort. 'Yes, Elad, enough of it. I prefer mixing it with water than with milk.'

Elad said, 'Try getting the organic grass-fed whey; I've heard, it's healthier.'

Elad was an Israeli who discovered Goa in his gap year after military service and decided to stay put in India, working as a personal trainer with MindCorp during the week and escaping to the beaches of Goa as often as he could.

Udai replied, 'Yes, I will put in a request with the HR to source some.'

Elad said, 'Yes, that works. Enough of the weight training; we are done with chest, shoulder, and triceps.' He flipped through a chart. 'To finish up, today is Krav Maga.'

Udai asked, 'Can't I just not be a non-violent Gandhian instead of an Israeli counter-terrorism street fighter today?'

Elad laughed, 'Well, they pay you a lot for this training, right? I doubt that starving yourself is going to get you that paycheck.'

Udai assumed position and Elad decided to spar with him. In a few seconds, Udai was flat on the floor. Elad said, 'Too much theory, Udai, and too little situational awareness. This isn't chess; you can't take your time to think. Trust your instincts. Come on, again.'

Udai assumed position again, and attacked. Once more, he was flat on the floor. Elad shook his head. 'Situational awareness, Udai. That's what you lack.'

'No, I am actually situationally quite aware. We are in an air-conditioned room, in a Fortune 500 company's premises. Forgive me, if I don't think I am in a real street fight.'

Elad wasn't going to relent, cheeky retorts notwithstanding. 'Again. You know I am going easy on you, because I owe you that money. If you have a problem with the air conditioning, I can take you in the sweltering heat to do some functional training. Do you fancy flipping tyres in the heat and the humidity?'

Udai replied, 'If you think I am going to cut you some slack if you go easy on me, you are highly mistaken.'

Elad said, 'I was kidding. You know I am good for it, right? You did save my life there, buddy.'

Udai winked at Elad. 'Have I ever asked for it? I have faith in you, Elad.'

'Thanks.'

As Udai once again assumed his position, their training was interrupted by a voice on the intercom—'Mr Udai Sodha, your presence is immediately required for a neural transfer. Please sanitize yourself and report to the neural bay, immediately.'

Udai shook his head. 'Whoa! Nothing was scheduled; it must be a sudden demise.' He looked at Elad. 'Next time, I am so going to kick your ass.'

Elad held his hands up and flipped him a finger, 'Situational awareness or not, at least, you have some positivity. Must be a Gandhian thing.'

Udai made his way into a pod, which vacuumed him clean. He then proceeded to wear a white tracksuit from Under Armour, and walked towards the neural bay.

He was greeted by the doctors, who were already in their surgical masks and wearing gloves. Udai winked at one of them, 'No heads up this time, huh? Thank you though, for saving me from the Krav Maga training.' He looked at the dead body, 'Looks pretty old, this guy.'

One of the doctors said, 'You know what that means.'

Udai winced, 'That's a fuck load of memories. Let's get on with it.'

He lay on the table next to the dead body. The doctor checked his eyes, and asked, 'Sanitized?'

Udai nodded. The doctor continued, 'And I assume that you've had no alcohol in the last 12 hours.' Udai gave a thumbs up. He was then hooked up to various machines; his blood pressure and heart rate were checked. A quick brain scan was done to ensure there was no minor injury either.

Finally, the doctor announced, 'Mr Udai Sodha is declared fit for a neural transfer from the decedent. Anaesthesia will now be administered and the transfer process will begin as soon as it kicks in.'

Udai shut his eyes as he watched the anaesthesiologist inject him. He winked at her once again and gave her a thumbs up. She smiled back. Udai started singing as the anaesthesia began working. His brain was then plugged into the neural network. The deceased person was already hooked up.

The doctor looked up at the technician. 'It's a greenlight. Begin the neural transfer; lots of memories, so keep the pace slow.' The technician pulled a lever and the neural network came alive, turning from red to green and the progress bar started. Estimated time showed '4 hours'. The doctor was a bit surprised. 'Wow—the guy sure had a lot on his mind. The longest I've seen is a two and a half hours estimate. Keep Udai monitored at all times; don't let his body temperature go above 100 degrees Fahrenheit. Any major changes in his vital signs and we might have to stop the transfer. It's going to be a long night.'

Home of the Chief of Army Staff, Delhi, India

The orderly was not even a bit apprehensive, as he forcefully knocked on the bedroom door of General Rodrigues. The General grunted something inaudible, acknowledging the knock. In a few minutes, the General was in the living room, clad in a t-shirt and trackpants. He stifled a yawn and asked, 'What is it, orderly?'

The orderly replied, 'Sir, the Southern Command in Pune wishes to speak to you immediately. Lt General Burman is on the line for you, sir.'

The Army Chief took the phone from the orderly before asking, 'Is it a secure connection?' The orderly nodded. Rodrigues checked the time on the massive wall clock—it was about 3:30 am. *Was that late night or early morning?* He could never tell. He spoke into the cell phone, 'Good morning, Burman. What's the issue?'

The voice at the other end was trying to conceal apprehension. 'Good morning, General. I am afraid, I have some bad news. It is about Ishtiaq Khan.'

The Army Chief cut him off. 'Jesus—did he try giving an interview again? We told him specifically not to engage in political gimmicks.'

He felt a slight quiver on the other side of the line. Or was it his imagination? 'It's not that, General. His wife called us. She believes that he was murdered.'

The General was alert now. 'Murdered? Someone murdered Ishtiaq Khan?' There was a hint of panic in his voice. He realized it too, but he couldn't let his subordinate know.

Lt General Burman said, 'That's not it, sir. His body was also taken.'

The General's voice tried to rein in the alarm bells, 'When did this happen?'

Burman replied, 'At least a few hours ago.'

'A few hours? He is supposed to have round-the-clock security.'

'Well, we were instructed not to keep a lot of security, just two guards. We wanted to install CCTVs all over, but Khan wanted his privacy and thought we would bug every room, so he insisted on minimal security. Having a retinue of guards outside would have alerted the locals. The idea is to keep his stay low profile.'

'The idea *was*, not *is*. The bloody bastard is dead. What about the guards?'

'They were not killed. Gagged and bound along with Khan's wife and placed inside the house. When the next shift guards came to relieve these chaps, they realized something was amiss.'

General Rodrigues, 'And she is sure that Khan has been murdered?'

'Yes, a hundred per cent.'

The General paused for an instant before saying, 'Be by the phone, Lt General, I am going to go and wake up the Defence Minister.'

MindCorp, Mumbai

The tall man was sitting unperturbed; it had been 2 hours since the brain transfer procedure had begun. As the first sign of impatience, he glanced at his wristwatch twice in a minute and then began tapping his foot. Noticing the change in his demeanour, Davis approached him. 'Can we arrange something for you, Mr Sinha? Perhaps you would like to use our high speed WiFi, or I could get you an iPad. We've got Netflix hooked up.'

The man smiled. 'How much longer will it take?'

'It really varies. But if I were a betting man, I would say that we are safely over the halfway mark.'

'I guess, then I shall take up on that offer of an iPad with Netflix. Could you also please arrange for a really strong black coffee?'

The man continued to surprise Davis. Sure, coffee was popular in India, but not black, and Indians still preferred their chai at all times, but he didn't bat an eyelid, and responded, 'Right away, Mr Sinha. I shall have both arranged ASAP.'

Office of the Defence Minister, South Block, New Delhi

The Defence Minister's eyes were red from lack of sleep, but to her credit, she had gotten to the office in less than 20 minutes. General Rodrigues was old-school, and initially, the chauvinist in him wasn't very happy to report to India's first woman Defence Minister. But thanks to her work ethic and ability to put people at ease, Ms Raman had begun to earn his grudging respect.

She was well-groomed as always, which struck him as inconceivable, given the amount of time his own wife and daughter took to get ready. Every Indian would always be a little chauvinistic and the General was no different. His thoughts were interrupted as the Defence Secretary, Mr Mishra, walked in. He was from the IAS Batch of 1985 and still dressed like it was 1985—in a ridiculous, ill-fitting safari suit, which made him look like an Indian version of Chairman Mao, with four cheap ball pens—two black, one blue, and one red—sticking out of his front pocket.

Ms Raman spoke in her signature soft voice. 'Yes, General Rodrigues, we are all here. You can tell us now, what is so important that it couldn't wait? Anything along the LoC, or the borders?'

The General shook his head. 'Not quite, Minister. Someone has murdered Khan.'

Mishra asked, 'Khan, as in Ishtiaq Khan, the Pakistani PM we are in the process of giving refugee status to?'

No, Genghis Khan, you imbecile bureaucrat, he thought, but said, 'Yes, the same.'

Mishra shook his head. The Minister's blood drained from her face. After the terror attacks, the opposition had been demanding her resignation. This was another fiasco.

She said, 'This has been a hell of a month. Has the press been informed?'

The General shook his head again. 'Nope, but there is another issue that's even graver.'

Mishra said, 'This just keeps getting better. What do you mean?'

The General continued, 'There is no easy way to say this, Minister. His body has been taken as well.'

Mishra said, 'What about the security?'

'The two guards—both are alive. In their statements they said that they were gassed, but they don't know who did this. When they woke up, they were gagged and bound. The guards in the next shift rescued them and Mrs Khan.'

The Minister asked, 'Just two guards?'

The General replied, 'Those were the instructions, madam. We had to keep his location low profile.'

Mishra asked, 'But where would they have taken his body?'

The General and the Defence Minister exclaimed in unison, 'MindCorp.'

The Defence Minister then turned to the Secretary, 'Mishra ji, get me the Chief Minister of Maharashtra and the Police Commissioner of Mumbai on the line, right now.'

Manama, Bahrain

As the middle-aged man sat smoking in the sauna, an attendant came in with a glass of freshly squeezed orange juice. Imagine sitting in a sauna, in a desert state, inside an air-conditioned hotel. Irony had no place in the Middle East. Everyone called him 'the Fixer'. He had a birth name, but very few people knew of it. He had multiple passports—all secured legally through actually buying citizenships—most of them from a bunch of Caribbean nations, which gave him access to travel visa-free to numerous countries. He had a Canadian passport too, but seldom used it—too much surveillance these days.

Fixer saw himself as a consultant. A consultant for multinational corporations, for drug lords from South America, and for rogue governments dodging sanctions. All of them wanted to get things done under the radar. He charged a flat fee of $500,000 per week, which of course had to be deposited in a bank in the Caribbean. Fixer had no political or religious affiliations. He was a capitalist, plain and simple. Every product or service had a price. Once that price was agreed upon between him and his client, he invariably delivered the desired result to his client. He was once asked, if there was any instance in history that he would have refused to fix. He had thought about it and said, 'If I had been paid to arrange for Che Guevara to be delivered to his killers, I wouldn't have done it. I've too much respect for the man.'

Some agencies knew of his existence and while collating data, one zealous recruit from the CIA had come up with the moniker 'the Fixer'; he liked it so much that he decided to use it professionally. He even contemplated getting visiting cards printed, but realized that it might be too dramatic. And no one who would want his services would need a visiting card. He was a ghost—no one would ever find his fingerprints on a smoking gun. He was the man who would supply the bullets for that gun and would teach the perp how and when to pull the trigger. He was 'the Consultant', 'the Fixer'.

He asked the attendant, 'Any word from Mumbai?'

The attendant replied, 'Nothing yet. But everything must be going according to plan, or else we would have heard something for sure.'

The man sipped his juice. 'For sure,' he mocked. 'Nothing ever goes according to plan. That's why we have to constantly monitor and be prepared for any hitches. Computer simulations can't predict everything.'

MindCorp, Mumbai, India

Trevor Davis was trying to get some shut-eye. He heard a knock on his door. *Clearly, an eventful night was in the offing*, he thought. 'Come in,' he said, as he expected his peon. Instead, it was his head of security—an appropriately military mannered and turbanned Sikh—Jasmeet Singh, a former army officer with a penchant for mouthing out-of-date British expressions. Not having time for any niceties, Singh shoved an iPad in Davis's face. He said, 'This isn't looking good, Mr Davis.'

Two security cams were visible: the first camera showed the lobby which had four cops, and a 360-degree view from the second drone camera showed that at the entrance, there stood another six odd cops, some of whom were armed. Davis was a bit taken aback by the show of force. Cops in Mumbai carried whistles and canes, not sophisticated weapons. But he assumed that it must have been triggered due to the recent terror attacks.

Singh said, 'The Senior Inspector has requested to see the person in charge here.'

Trevor nodded his head. 'Right away.'

He left his office as Singh followed him. He approached the portly Senior Inspector who, clearly, wasn't very happy to be on red-eye duty. His name tag said 'R.P. Deshpande.' Davis knew better than to mispronounce the name of an official, so he was guardedly neutral. Davis thrust his hand forward as he said, 'Yes, Inspector.'

The Inspector lethargically shook Davis's hand and asked, 'Have there been any sudden, unexpected admissions in the last few hours?'

Davis knew that he was going to be in hot water. *I should not have pocketed the extra dough*, he thought. 'Yes, as a matter of fact, an unannounced and unexpected subject was brought in for processing earlier this evening.'

Inspector Deshpande was almost disappointed—this meant more work. 'What time did they leave?'

Davis said, 'I am afraid, you don't understand. The body is currently in processing.'

Deshpande perked up. 'The body is still here?'

Singh chimed in, 'Yes, currently the transfer is on.'

Deshpande continued, 'Well then, you need to take me there and we need to stop the transfer.'

A voice boomed, 'It cannot be stopped.'

All of them turned to see Sinha, who threw something in their direction. Singh immediately realized what it was from the odour. 'Bloody hell! It is tear gas. Everyone, get down.'

But Sinha wasn't done yet; he started firing in the general direction of the smoke. Davis, Singh, and the cops instinctively ducked for cover behind various pieces of furniture amidst bouts of coughing, while trying to see through the smoke with tear filled eyes.

Davis turned to the Inspector and managed to mumble, 'Can't you shoot back?'

Deshpande held up his oldish looking service revolver right at Davis's nose, 'I can't see through the smoke. What if I hit one of your employees?'

Davis desperately asked his head of security, 'What about you?'

'I had bloody well asked for some protective gear; you ordered a pepper spray and a box of Durex for me from Amazon.'

Sinha marched towards the operating room. He unlocked his cell phone and sent a WeChat message, 'Contingency Plan A'. He opened the door of the operation theatre where the neural transfer was taking place. The six staff members had been insulated from the sounds outside, and looked at him with disdain.

The doctor said, 'No one is allowed in here.'

Sinha whipped out his gun. 'How much of the transfer is left?'

The doctor looked at his staff; frozen. The doctor mumbled, 'The transfer is done, but the cooling process takes some time.'

'Unfortunately, we don't have the time. Get your man out.'

A nurse rushed and said, 'But that is not possible.'

Sinha did not blink. He shot her right in the head. As the body slumped, the man said, 'I won't ask again.'

The rest of the staff unhooked Udai from the network, as the doctor mumbled, 'I don't know what you are doing.'

Sinha said, 'It is better for you that way.' Udai was groggy. His head felt heavy.

Holding Udai in one arm, Sinha looked up his chart and noted his name. He sent another WeChat message, 'Udai Singh Sodha', to his contact and whispered in Udai's ear. 'I need to get you out of here. Don't panic.'

He looked at various operation theatre masks lying on the table and put one over his own mouth and one over Udai's. He then put on a doctor's spare coat and made the groggy Udai wear one as well. He directed the rest of the staff in the operation theatre to do the same. 'If I see even one of you remove your masks, I will shoot you.' He removed his gun and shot in the air—'Now run for your life!'

As the five staff members started running outside, there was massive commotion in the reception and lounge area, where the smoke had begun to settle. One of the operation theatre nurses shouted, 'He shot Sheila! He shot Sheila!' Before the cops could gather their wits, the remaining staff members heard the commotion and started running towards the exit. A significant number of them had masks on.

The cops waiting outside were overwhelmed as they saw the crowd rush towards them. They immediately began to glance inside to see what was happening. Amidst the confusion, the tall man led Udai to a parked brown coloured Suzuki Wagon R, one of the most common cars in India. It easily blended into the general traffic, thus was always harder to trace. He tapped the driver on the shoulder, 'Vantage Point.'

Office of the Defence Minister, South Block, New Delhi

Lt General Burman was stroking his eyebrow as he was watched on the screen by the Defence Minister, the Chief of Army Staff, and Secretary Mishra.

Burman said, 'The only positive news from Mumbai is that we were able to recover Khan's body.'

Mishra said, 'After the transfer was complete. And the man—what's his name...?' he looked at his memo pad—'Udai Singh Sodha. This man has all the memories of Khan.'

Burman, 'Yes, it seems so.'

The Defence Minister interjected, 'And why did you let the police force handle this? This required careful military planning.'

Burman replied, 'Madam, it is a matter of jurisdiction. I can't send in the army into a civilian area unless a law like AFSPA† is in place. This is Mumbai, not Kashmir.'

General Rodrigues nodded. 'He is right, Minister. The cops should have been more competent.'

The Defence Minister sighed and said, 'This is not the time to point fingers. Now, what is the status update?'

Burman replied, 'We spoke to the MindCorp head here in Mumbai. He is an American expatriate named Trevor Davis. He says that this Udai chap currently holds simultaneously not only Khan's memories, but also his own.'

The Minister countered, 'And what does that mean for us?'

Burman continued, 'The human brain is not equipped for that. He will hemorrhage and his brain can shut down anytime. What most likely will follow is multiple organ failure. But no one is sure.'

Mishra asked, 'What do you mean?'

Burman, 'They clearly have never anticipated anything of this nature. Their premises in all their locations across the globe are backed up with three electric back up units, so the worst case scenario for them was a massive power failure of a grid and of a backup generator. They had not anticipated a kidnapping of the mind of a politician in the middle of the process.'

Mishra said, 'This is a completely bizarre situation. We can't have such sensitive political information falling into the hands

---

† Armed Forces (Special Powers) Acts (AFSPA), 1958, are Acts of the Parliament of India that grant special powers to the Indian Armed Forces the power to maintain public order in 'disturbed areas'.

of an enemy state. We need to get hold of this Udai chap ASAP.' He reluctantly added, 'Dead, or alive.'

The Minister arched her eyebrows, 'Dead, or alive?'

Mishra said, 'Well, it is the mind of a Pakistani Prime Minister in refuge in the body of a civilian. It possibly has state secrets—secrets which we need and we can't have them fall into the hands of an enemy state.'

The Defence Minister said, 'Yes, and tell that to the family of this Udai Sodha. And the press would have a field day. I am barely keeping my head above the water. Another crisis and I will be relegated to some useless ministry like the Ministry of Food Processing Industries, or some such.'

Secretary Mishra interjected, 'We are at the horns of another dilemma.'

The Defence Minister snapped, 'What else now?'

Mishra said, 'Jurisdiction.'

The General groaned. 'Trust a bureaucrat to inject red tape in this situation as well. What do you mean?'

Mishra said, 'There are two minds in one body. One is of a foreigner, and the other one is of a citizen.'

The General said, 'Thank you, but we already know that.'

Mishra ignored the barb. 'So is this a matter for RAW which deals with foreigners, or for the CBI which deals with domestic issues? If he does leak information and we catch him, will he be tried as a foreigner, or will he be tried as a citizen?'

The Defence Minister looked ill at ease. 'I don't know... It is a peculiar situation.'

Mishra countered, 'Ideally, in such a situation, we should seek the input of the Law Ministry through a white paper!'

The General laughed. 'You are bloody insane, Mishra. Why don't we give the Law Ministry a three-year deadline to submit a white paper, and then form a committee to give its expert opinion on the white paper? Then our super-efficient Parliament can discuss the issue, when they are not disrupting the House. Don't be ridiculous.'

Mishra said, 'What do we do then?'

The General replied, 'We cut through the bullshit and the red tape. We get someone from RAW to handle the case considering this has international implications. There is no doubting the competency of the CBI, but we just need to work fast on this. We can't allow this Udai fellow to get away, while we discuss procedure!'

Mishra countered, 'But that would be circumventing the process...'

The Defence Minister cut in, 'No, it wouldn't. It would mean streamlining the process. I like the General's idea. General, do you have someone in mind from RAW, someone deputed by the Armed Forces?'

The General replied, 'As a matter of fact, I do.'

On the Arabian Sea Coastline, Daman, India

Udai felt an icy jolt, as cold water was splashed on his face. He tried to move his hands to wipe his face only to realize that his hands were tied. He tried to wriggle free, but the knot was pretty tight. A *fisherman's knot*, he could recall from his Boy Scout days. He shook his head violently to shake the water off and immediately let out a small cry as his head hurt.

Worst hangover ever. No, I wasn't drinking last night. I was in the middle of a transfer. Someone yanked me off. God. Where the fuck am I?

He slowly opened his eyes to see the a tall man before him. The man had an impassive face. Neither was he smiling, nor was he frowning. He had the look of a patient man. Udai found that his voice was still groggy as he managed to mutter, 'Who are you? Where am I?'

'I am terribly sorry about this.' The man's apology had an unmistakable ring of sincerity.

Udai asked, 'What exactly did you do?'

'I brought you in from MindCorp. You were in the midst of a transfer. Actually, I think the transfer was complete.' He hesitated a moment. 'Actually, I am pretty sure it was complete.'

The colour drained from Udai's face. His tone switched from being confused to being accusatory and aggressive. 'Sorry about yanking me off in the middle of the transfer? Or kidnapping me? Or tying me up?'

The man had a wry smile now; he twirled his fingers to make an imaginary globe.

'It was really a holistic apology.'

'Am I supposed to say, *I forgive you*?'

'No, I guess not. Not yet, anyway. You can do that once we spare you.'

'We? Who are *we*?'

The man held Udai's shoulders. 'I know, you are smart. I've been through your file. Mensa level IQ—different tests show either in the upper 130s or lower 140s. You will eventually figure it out and put the pieces together.'

The invasion of personal space made Udai even more uneasy. 'What do you want?'

'Come on, you know it.' The man tapped on Udai's head. 'That's 24 carat gold for us.'

Udai said, 'Yes, but you can't do it in India. You will have to take me to a different country. You can't fly out, so the option is either via road or sea. If it were via road, we would be at a higher altitude in the north, or through the desert in the west—neither of which is true. The air is too thick to be on a higher altitude and it is not hot enough to be anywhere near the desert. So I take it that we are somewhere on the Western Coast, waiting for a boat which can slip by the coast guard?'

The man clapped twice. 'Fuckin' awesome. It is like watching a live episode of Sherlock on Netflix. It's like I am Watson and I have a ringside view.'

'Want an autograph?'

'I would, but I've tied your hands, haven't I?'

Udai raised his eyebrows. 'Am I a flight risk?'

The man untied him, 'I guess not. I had chosen another name at the MindCorp office, but you obviously know that is not my name. And since we are going to be joined at the hip for a while, you should call me Watson.'

'More like Waqar, no?'

The man shook his head and wagged his finger in a paternal manner. 'Stop taxing that overworked brain of yours. It might burst, literally, considering you are carrying the minds of two people in there.'

Watson removed a hotspot and switched it on. The LED lights blinked green. Cell phone signals could be traced, but stolen hotspots were gold dust, even if they used the same signal. They were not as critical as cell phones, so people seldom reported them stolen. They assume that they have misplaced the device, or they just go buy a new one. He switched on a fresh cell phone and connected to the hotspot. He then made a VoIP call to the Fixer, who replied with a curt, 'Yes?'

'We are at Vantage Point A.'

'You will be picked up soon. Wait for the next message.' The Fixer disconnected the phone.

Watson looked at Udai. 'Relief is on its way.'

Udai looked at him, trying not to blink. 'You think you can just kidnap an Indian citizen working for a major American corporation and get away? The public outcry right now should concern you.'

Watson said, 'It should have, had there been a public outcry. You are not on the news right now.'

'I don't believe you.'

'I don't blame you, but here, see for yourself.' Watson put his cell phone in front of Udai's face and played a YouTube clip from a news channel.

The anchor spoke, 'There have been unconfirmed reports of an incident at the MindCorp office in Mumbai. Residents living nearby claim that they heard gunshots, and there's a footage shot by a resident from a residential tower nearby showing a horde of people coming out of the office.' Then the video showed a grainy footage of people rushing out. 'When contacted, both the local police station and the MindCorp spokesperson declined to comment. Since this is a developing story, we will continue with the updates.'

Watson smiled. 'See, no mention of you.'

Udai appeared confused, 'But why?'

'Come on, Sherlock, don't disappoint me. Why do you think?' Watson was clearly enjoying the taunting.

'Something important in the old man's memories—something of national importance. The Indian Government can't afford to let the information fall into the wrong hands.'

'No shit, Sherlock. And it is not just of national importance, also of international importance.'

Udai started coughing. 'I need water.'

'Yes, we need to keep you hydrated.' Watson removed a bottle of water from his bag and handed it over.

Even as Udai was sipping water, Watson walked over to a portable ice box and handed him an ice pack. 'I've been told that this will help cool your head. Keep applying it. I have lots of ice packs. You shall need it.'

Udai exclaimed, 'I think I know who it is.'

Watson was curious. 'From the memories? Or an educated guess?'

Udai said, 'Guess, I think. I can't access the memories. It's the Pakistani Prime Minister, Ishtiaq Khan, isn't it? That would explain the secrecy and the sheer amount of data that needed to be processed.'

Watson winked, but did not reply in the affirmative. He did not need to.

Udai replied, 'Are we going far?'

Watson smiled. 'Man, if this is how your brain works, when it is not optimally performing, I shudder to think how it does, when you are not groggy and sedated.'

Gamdevi Police Station, Mumbai

The Sub-Inspector had heard the story far too many times to actually trouble herself with bringing pen to paper to jot down an FIR. She smiled at the well-groomed SoBo lady, who seemed anxious, 'Husband is missing, madam?'

'Yes. I have already told you.'

'Madam, are you sure he didn't go drinking with his friends and stayed with one of them? *Boyz nite hota hai na kabhi kabhi...*'

'*Nahi, woh kaam pe thay*. He often works through the night and comes home at 6 in the morning.'

'Call centre?' The cop was surprised. This lady definitely looked a few notches higher on the economic scale than the wife of a call centre employee.

'No!'

'Toh chowkidar hai kay?' The cop laughed.

The complainant was not amused. She simply said, 'MindCorp.'

The cop's smile disappeared; she said, '*Thamba*. I will be right back.'

As Aditi Sodha waited in a room whose ancient fan creaked along, she sweated profusely. She didn't care; she would wait as long as it took.

The cop returned with her smile back in place, after 15 odd minutes. 'Madam, I've spoken to the ACP. You write down everything and give it to me. Something weird went down in MindCorp last night—that's for certain. We will get back to you. Please write down your phone number in the complaint.'

She quickly jotted down her number, not seriously expecting any call back. She knew it was she who would have to follow up. That's just how things worked around here.

Embassy of the People's Republic of China, Islamabad, Pakistan

Except for photo-ops, Pakistan was used to the civilian leadership reporting to the top military brass. It was usually the Pakistani Prime Minister who would go to the Army GHQ in the nearby town of Rawalpindi. It had been a while since a military chief was answerable to civilians. The General took solace from the fact that at least, he was not reporting to a Pakistani civilian.

The Chinese Ambassador, Jie Huang, had enjoyed the confidence of the Communist Party back at home and had held the post for a few years now. Many saw him as the architect of the recent Chinese takeover. Officially, the Chinese were not calling it an invasion: it was termed as a 'Brotherly Intervention'.

The official line was that as an elder brother often has to lend a helping hand to a misdirected younger sibling, China too was doing the same. No one pointed out that Pakistan was formed in 1947 and the People's Republic of China in 1948. In Pakistani circles, the facade was already crumbling. The common people and sections of the press had started referring to Huang as 'Viceroy Huang', instead of 'Ambassador Huang'. It didn't bother Huang too much, as he was focused on his country's priorities, not on appeasing the vocal fringe in Pakistan. Considering most of the country was illiterate, hero-worshipped the military, and loved the Chinese people as messiahs, he could not care less about what the English press, which catered to a small Westernized liberal elite, wrote.

General Ahmed greeted him with a firm handshake. 'You requested a meeting, Mr Ambassador?' It was hardly a request. And both of them knew that. But the game always must be played, even within closed doors.

'Yes, General Ahmed. Thank you for coming. May I offer you some tea?'

The General had a penchant for a good Scotch. But it was not going to be offered. He removed his pack of Marlboro Lights. 'No thank you. But I am sure, you won't mind if I smoke.' He didn't wait for a reply and lit one up.

Ambassador Huang politely smiled. 'Very well. I shall get straight to the point then. The recent attacks in India—do you or any of your people have anything to do with it?'

The General shrugged his shoulders. 'Not that I know of.'

The Ambassador dropped the smile. 'That doesn't sound very convincing.' He sat at his own desk, pulled the cigarette from the General's hand, and stubbed it on the floor, not caring about the carpet. 'Let me level with you, General. We are here to protect the investments and the rights of the People's Republic of China. Your country is bankrupt. We have poured billions into your country via OBOR[‡] and CPEC[§]. We are here not as rulers, but as guides. We will leave once we protect and secure our interests. What we don't need, nor desire, is to get into a military conflict with India.'

The General was taken aback. 'Together we can easily take on India, if they attack us. You alone are capable of doing so.'

The Ambassador shook his head. 'Let's just think about that. Our forces are spread thin. India is a strategic ally of USA and Russia—I don't know of any country which manages to keep both of them as close friends. They have quite possibly the best navy in Asia. But all of that is not even the point.'

The General bit the bait. 'Then what is the point?'

The Ambassador continued, 'The point is that we don't live in the 19th century. Chinese telecom and hardware manufacturers have set up plants in India. India supplies pharmaceuticals and software to China. They are one of our biggest trading partners and export markets. Indian kids are more familiar with Xiaomi and Huawei than with Apple and Microsoft. Some Bollywood movies make more money in China than in India. Our economies are increasingly intertwined.

‡ The One Belt One Road (OBOR), also known as the Belt and Road Initiative (BRI), or the Silk Road Economic Belt and the 21st-century Maritime Silk Road, is a development strategy adopted by the Chinese government involving infrastructure development and investments in 152 countries and international organizations in Europe, Asia, Middle East, Latin America, and Africa.

§ The China–Pakistan Economic Corridor (CPEC) is a collection of ongoing infrastructure projects, which aims to connect the Gwadar Port of Pakistan to China's northwestern region of Xinjiang, via a network of highways, railways, and pipelines. The economic corridor is considered central to China–Pakistan relations and will run about 2700 km from Gwadar to Kashghar.

What's more, we have a massive trade surplus with India. Why would we want to go to war with India?'

The General fumbled. 'I don't know.' He saw the door slide open, and the Chinese military attaché, Colonel Lin, joined the meeting. The Ambassador acknowledged his arrival with a slight tilt of the head as he said, 'Shang Xiao Lin.' The diminutive Chinese officer offered a slight smile to both the men. Ahmed knew there was always friction in the military and the civilian leadership of China. If the Ambassador represented the interests of the Communist Party, Lin was the man who represented the People's Army.

The Ambassador continued, 'I really did not want an answer there, General. We don't want to go to war with India. So, if there are elements within Pakistan who are responsible for those terror attacks in India, you will let me know within the week.'

The General wasn't giving up. 'They offered refuge to Ishtiaq Khan and his entire coterie, and even to the disloyal members from the Air Force and Navy.'

The Ambassador replied, 'Loyalty is a matter of perspective, General. From your perspective perhaps they are disloyal. And yes, India did offer refuge to your opponents. But they didn't have a choice. They always offer refuge to people and Khan caught them off guard. Now level with me—are your people involved in those terror attacks?'

'I really don't know. But what will you do with them, if they are?'

'As we bloody well deem fit.' Once again the General was taken aback. The Ambassador softened his tone a bit. 'General Ahmed, you are my man here. We are working together towards a common goal—the success of Chinese investments and the upliftment of the Pakistani people. We stay happy, you stay happy. If the goal changes, that will not augur too well for either of us. I, as the Ambassador, might be replaced by a military general from the People's Army. And he might feel the need to find a replacement for you as well.'

The General got up and nodded. 'I will get back to you soon.' He hesitated; he had never saluted a civilian before. But he clicked his heels and did so this time.

Research and Analysis Wing (RAW), New Delhi, India

Mayank was thinking of popping a Crocin for the headache, when his desk phone buzzed and he was summoned to the Director's room.

The Director's room was as nondescript as the rest of the RAW building; one of the last vestiges of India's close ties to the erstwhile Soviet Union with its 1960s' frugal architecture. Unlike other intelligence services, like the CIA and Mossad, RAW was not an independent organization. It was an extension of the Prime Minister's Office, the PMO, so it did not need to report to anyone except to the Prime Minister.

The Director gestured towards an empty chair in what was already a crowded room. He said, 'Major Mayank Bose, you obviously know General Rodrigues and Lt General Burman. And this here is Mr Mishra, the Defence Secretary.'

He saluted his two military superiors and then firmly shook the hands of all three men. 'Good evening, generals, and Mr Mishra. How may I be of assistance?'

Mr Mishra smiled. 'Your accent has the bearings of a fancy school, Mr Bose. Are you a fellow Dosco from Doon?'

Bose shook his head. 'I am afraid not. I went to Mayo and then straight to the National Defence Academy.'

Mishra said, 'Yes, yes, of course. I read your file. Must have slipped my mind.'

Bose smiled. *Nothing slips your mind, if you are the top bureaucrat in the Defence Ministry*. Bose asked again, 'So, what can I do for you, sirs?'

General Rodrigues spoke, 'Well, Major, it is a matter of urgency—'

Bose held up his hand and removed his cell phone. He whipped out a stylus and asked, 'Do you mind, if I take notes?' His superiors looked at each other.

Mishra said, 'By all means, do take notes. It's good that you're meticulous. This is going to be quite complex. You have heard about what happened in Mumbai, right?'

Bose nodded.

Rodrigues said, 'Well, Major, this is what we need you to do...'

Off the coast of India, the Arabian Sea

Even as his head throbbed, Udai was trying to figure out what was going on. *I should have joined some bank. Fuck this—no time to feel sorry*.

Watson interrupted his thoughts. 'Need some more ice? Or some pain killer?'

The pills are making me drowsy, I need to be alert, he realized. 'Just give me some ice.'

Watson laughed. 'It's almost as if you have ordered a drink and not enough ice has been served.' Despite his visceral hatred for the man, Udai cracked a smile.

'Where are you taking me? Surely we can't go very far in a fishing trawler.'

'Of course, we can't. Look toward the horizon.' There was a larger ship flying what looked like a Norwegian flag.

Udai gave him a quizzical look. 'Norwegian flag? Really?'

Watson shrugged in response. 'No one stops or bothers Scandinavian ships.'

'Except Somali pirates.'

'Yeah. Fuck! That slipped my mind. I guess we will take our chances. Trust me, we have more weapons than a Scandinavian merchant ship would carry. Do you want some tea?'

Udai shook his head. 'What are you? Does your kid give you a trophy for the "Most Hospitable Kidnapper Dad in the World"?'

Makeshift Police Office, Mumbai, India

Mayank had been told that he was being given an 'office'. He had seen slums that were roomier. To top it, the office was located near a busy traffic intersection with incessant honking and no sound proofing. He couldn't wait to get back to Delhi, where space was never a problem. At least, it wasn't for government officers. In Mumbai, space was always something you compromised on and settled for.

He had asked for a whiteboard with pens. Instead he was presented with an ancient blackboard with chalk. As his assistant, Inspector Rao, showed him an entire box of multi-coloured chalk, Mayank shot him a resigned look. He removed one of the chalks and started using the blackboard.

'Inspector Rao, we have to get to this Udai Sodha fellow. Let's discuss what we know.' He began writing—

1. China invaded Pakistan and overthrew the govt.
2. Deposed PM Khan seeks refuge in India
3. A series of terror attacks all over India
4. Pak PM is murdered in India
5. His body and memories stolen

He looked at Rao and said, 'Now let's try connecting the dots. What does this tell us?'

Rao said, 'I don't think that the Chinese would greenlight a terror attack on Indian soil; they have too much on their plate. So could it be those who were loyal to Khan?'

Mayank shook his head. 'That's based on an assumption that Pakistanis conducted those terror raids. The bloody media has conditioned even us to think like that.'

'So you are saying it isn't them?'

'All I am saying is that an investigation starts with a clean slate. Prime Minister Khan had only been given interim refuge. In my meeting with the superiors, I was told that Khan had something to barter for complete and permanent political asylum. Something major.'

'What was it?'

'He didn't say. He wanted to secure permanent political asylum first and our government wanted to know what he had to offer first. He was more desperate, so the government was willing to wait. They were sure he would blink first. His last assurance was that it would alter the course of history.'

'And now that information is in Udai Sodha's head?'

'Exactly!'

'So who is that information valuable to?' Rao asked.

Mayank opened a map on his desktop and started pointing at countries. 'It is valuable to India. It is valuable to Pakistan and its new master China. It could be valuable to the Americans. Russia has always had an interest in the region since the Afghan War of the 1970s and it hates Pakistan.'

Rao, 'And it could also be a bluff?'

Mayank stated, 'Unlikely. His refugee status would have been revoked. Khan wouldn't put his neck on the line.'

'What would happen, if the refugee status got revoked?'

'We would have to hand him over back to the current Pakistani dispensation. There he would likely be hanged under some charge or another. Or he could go to the UN offices here and apply for refuge. Or he could go to any South American or Scandinavian Embassy in New Delhi.'

'Wouldn't that be a better option for him than sticking around in India?'

'No. Because no one—and I mean no one—wants to piss off the Chinese. We wanted to hand him over ASAP, but no country was willing to offer him refuge. Not even the Saudis.'

Rao asked, 'So any stakeholder could have conducted or engineered the terror attacks in India to prevent Khan's asylum? And then, when we didn't eject him, one of them killed him to take his memories?'

Mayank replied, 'Not just that—they either want his memories or they want to ensure the memories don't fall into India's hands.'

Rao looked around the room. 'So we are supposed to investigate USA, China, Russia, and Pakistan out of this dump?'

Mayank sighed, 'Evidently. Get a bloody whiteboard, and get some soundproofing foam. And I need a few constables to run errands as well. Make a few calls to the local commissioner.'

Embassy of People's Republic of China, Islamabad, Pakistan

If Ambassador Huang was angry with Colonel Lin, he certainly did not show it. 'Colonel Lin, is there any particular reason you gatecrashed a meeting with General Ahmed?'

Lin feigned ignorance. 'I didn't realize that this was a secret meeting.'

'It wasn't and you know it. What's the report on the ground? Any progress?'

'Yes, but it is at snail's pace compared to what we are used to back home.'

The Ambassador frowned. 'Why? The Pakistanis have assured us of full cooperation.'

Colonel Lin shook his head vigorously. 'Where do I even begin?' He whipped out his cell phone and showed a video to the Ambassador. It was a scuffle between Chinese soldiers and Pakistani soldiers even as ordinary Pakistani citizens looked on, with expressions ranging from bemused to shell shocked.

The Ambassador gave the colonel a quizzical look.

The Colonel said, 'This is in KPK province, just outside of Peshawar. Some of our workers on the bridge, after their shift, wanted to visit the local red light district. They were prevented from doing so by the Pakistani soldiers. The Pakistanis told them that the area is infested with Taliban and their supporters. So our workers started beating up their soldiers. Soon, the Pakistani soldiers started beating them back and someone called a local Chinese platoon which joined the scuffle.'

The Ambassador threw up his hands. 'You are coming to me because your workers and soldiers can't get to the local whores?'

The Colonel replied, 'I don't think you understand. My people don't like being here. The local Pakistanis certainly don't like us being here. Not like we expected. There is a major cultural chasm. There are no malls, no beaches, and no movie halls. They hate the local cuisine. It is like a forced marriage.' The Ambassador opened his drawer and spread a map on the desk. He pointed to the grandiose Chinese vision to create a new Silk Route. 'This is the One Belt One Road initiative.' He then pointed to various red lines on the Pakistani part of the map. 'And the China-Pakistan Economic Corridor is a critical cog in our plans. We are trying to build a system, which would serve as an alternative to the American and Western dominated trade system.' He neatly wrapped up the map and placed it back in the drawer. 'Am I to report to Beijing that we should abandon our ambitious plans to rival the United States, because Colonel Lin's workers can't get to the local whores?'

The Colonel shook his head again. 'I didn't say that. You Ambassador, are the politician. Those are my soldiers on the ground. Strategic objectives can't be achieved amidst a hostile population. My army here isn't dealing with self-immolating Buddhist monks. It is dealing with off-shoots of Taliban and ISIS who have years and years of war experience. They are excellent guerilla fighters.'

'What would you have me do to ease it for you? Lest you forget we are on the same side.'

'I did not say we are not on the same side.'

The Ambassador continued, 'No, you did not. But you did insinuate it. Do you think when countries like Britain conquered and built infrastructure in India and Africa, they did not face issues? They built railways in Asia and Africa—you see their mark everywhere from India to Kenya. So too with the French and their colonial possessions.'

The Colonel raised his eyebrows, 'Are we colonizers then?'

The Ambassador gathered his thoughts. 'Not in the 19th century sense of the word. But we don't need complete control on the political system anymore, like the British and the French did. In the 21st century, everyone is an economic colony of the United States. Google, Apple, Microsoft, Cisco, Facebook, Twitter—these are the American tools of colonization today. We are weaning them off the American dream and giving them an alternative. A Chinese alternative which would make China the predominant economic power in the world eventually.

Maybe not in our lifetimes, but with over a billion people, it is our destiny.'

'But India too has over a billion people.'

'Which is a problem. With their Buddhism, Yoga, and Bollywood, they have more soft power than all of our initiatives like Confucius Institutes have been able to muster. Ethnic Indians also become top politicians in the US and the UK. We must always be wary of them. Which brings me to my next question.'

'Which is?'

'Do we know who was responsible for the attacks in India?'

The Colonel's face was expressionless. 'We don't. But every attack of this scale on India in the last 30 odd years tends to have Pakistani fingerprints all over it.'

The Ambassador gritted his teeth before regaining his composure. 'Well, Pakistanis are not in control of their country at the moment. We are. I have a meeting with the Indian High Commissioner, an informal one. I will assure him of our full cooperation. If some Pakistani idiots think they can derail our Silk Road initiative, or use us as a shield while attacking India, they are mistaken. We will hand them over. And let the Pakistanis twiddle their thumbs. Are we both on the same page?'

The Colonel stood up and put forth his hand. 'I assure you the People's Army is always with you. We will do all we can.'

The Ambassador and the General shook on it.

MindCorp, Mumbai, India

Trevor Davis was on a Skype conference call with the Head of Asia-Pacific, based in Singapore, and a range of individuals at CxO level based in California. He had been getting pounded via e-mail. Now it was time to get pounded via video chat. He really needed some sleep.

Some of the management wanted him to seek counseling as he may be traumatized. Some thought that he was being too greedy by not completing the vetting process of the stranger who brought in Khan's body. *Hindsight is a wonderful thing.* If he wasn't so exhausted, it would even be amusing—Corporate America with its deadlines, bottom lines, marketing gimmicks, and stock value acting like a tree-hugging Scandinavian company which cared deeply about Mother Earth and all her children. *Cry me a fucking river*, he said to himself.

As he ended the Skype call, he asked his Security Head, Singh, to come in.

Davis asked, 'Do we have any information at all on Udai?'

Singh shook his head. 'The police are either deliberately stalling, or they genuinely don't know anything. His wife keeps asking for you.'

'Yes, that is both unavoidable and unfortunate. Set up a meeting in one of our cozy conference rooms. Actually, on second thought, this place might be traumatic for her. Or she might create a scene. Set up a meeting in a Starbucks.'

Singh smirked. 'That great American soul saver and cheap shrink.'

'Fuckin-A, Singh. I got enough shit today from my superiors. I don't need any lip from you.'

Karachi, Pakistan

After a while, you get used to it, Udai thought. *Or maybe your mind just adapts.* His head was still throbbing and he was in pain, but he was getting used to it. It didn't mean that his brain could sustain the sheer rigour of this stress though. The last thing he wanted was to hemorrhage, but none of this was in his control anymore. He *hated* that.

Watson had been injecting him with all sorts of chemicals, assuring him that those would help. Udai had no idea whether Watson got that information from a brain surgeon or a quack, but he didn't care anymore, as Watson handed him some 'anti-inflammation' pills.

Udai said, 'Watson, I really don't give a fuck about you and your geopolitics. Just get me to a damn MindCorp centre and take your information. I don't care. I won't even step into a MindCorp office again.'

Watson nodded. 'Listen, for what it's worth, I am sorry. I know this is a tough situation for you.'

'Stop acting like you are Karan Johar from that godforsaken show.'

'Koffee with Karan?'

'No shit. Stop the empathy and get me out of here.'

'Listen Udai. There are no MindCorp centres in Karachi, or in Pakistan, for that matter. We need to take you to a centre close by. We are working it out. We could bring you in because of the vast Pakistani coastline. We can't do that in other countries. We need that information as badly as you need to keep your mind safe. So hang in there.'

'I can help. Just run the scenarios by me.'

Watson was genuinely taken aback. 'Wow! That must be a first. You want to help your kidnapper. I guess, it is only logical.'

'Yes, it is.'

'Don't tax that brain of yours. We will get you out ASAP.'

Makeshift Police Office, Mumbai, India

The premises had finally begun to resemble an office. Mayank scanned the room. They had computers, a few hotspot devices, a whiteboard, and most importantly, sound absorbing foam.

The local police chief had lent him four constables available around the clock, in 12-hour shifts of two each.

His thoughts were interrupted as Rao tapped him on the shoulder. Mayank turned around. 'Yes?'

Rao handed him a file. Mayank started flipping through it. It was a bit thinner than he had expected. *Which might mean the guy was low on experience or that he might be a good spook.* 'This is our man for Pakistan, then? How long has he been in service?'

Rao nodded. 'About seven years now. He is our best bet. He will fly under the radar. But his field experience has been in South East Asia and the Far East.'

'Yes, given his background, that is not surprising. Where is his family?'

'Chang is from Tangra; he is more of a Calcutta boy than you are. I think you will like him.'

'I like everyone, Rao. Even you. Now, what's his cover?'

Islamabad, Pakistan

The officer at the Emigration counter at the Islamabad International Airport looked at the Canadian passport and then glanced at the Chinese man standing in front of her. The passport was filled with lots of official looking stamps. She looked for a valid Pakistani visa. Having found it, she asked, 'Purpose of visit to Pakistan, Mr Chang?'

Chang offered her a smile. 'Business. CPEC.'

That was enough. Without further questions, his passport was stamped. *Well, these days Pakistan is almost a Chinese colony*, he thought. *The officials would have no choice but to be polite, even servile to anyone Chinese.*

But of course he had never felt Chinese. Ethnically, yes, there always had been some mean kids around, who would refer to him as 'Chinky'¶, but he didn't feel any affection towards the Communist State. The eighth last generation of his family had settled around the Chinatown area in Tangra, Calcutta. Once a strong community of almost 50,000, the number of ethnic Chinese in India had begun to dwindle. Most sought greener pastures in Western nations. The few that remained were such a drop in a country of 1.3 billion that they barely even registered. Perhaps that was the reason why he was recruited after completing his military training. Ethnically Chinese, his family was as Indian as they come. For the Intelligence Agencies, he was as rare as an ice cube in the Sahara. On this mission, he had considered using another name, but 'Chang' was common enough. Whether you opened a directory in Shanghai or in San Francisco, there was never a dearth of Changs. He wagered it would be the same in Pakistan. So 'Robert Chang', the Chinese-Canadian businessman, would blend right in.

He had been briefed that he would be accosted by cab drivers right outside the terminal. He obviously would take no chance. He booked an Uber from his smartphone and politely refused the cab driver brigade that continued to badger him till the Uber arrived. He had inserted the destination as 'Islamabad Serena Hotel', reputed to be the best hotel in Pakistan. Good thing that the Government of India was bankrolling a luxurious stay. His usual operations involved drug smugglers in Asia, and he had stayed at some pretty seedy places, which would make even YMCA hostels look luxurious.

¶ 'Chinky' is an English-language ethnic slur usually referring to a person of Chinese ethnicity. The word is also sometimes indiscriminately used against people of East Asian appearance. The use of the term is considered offensive.

Unfortunately, the brief was to keep the mission as short as possible. As an Indian, he got to lord it over the Pakistanis, even if he was posing as a Chinese. He could happily do it for a pretty long time. The thought amused him and he allowed himself a slight chuckle.

As they entered the hotel, he noticed that the security was incredibly tight. There were multiple layers of checkpoints and everyone was being thoroughly checked. Much to his disappointment, being a 'Chinese' did not get him a free pass either. It was understandable though. The Taliban and ISIS country was not too far away, and Islamabad, or *Isloo*, as the locals called it, was packed with diplomats, politicians, and businessmen. And the Serena was the vortex, where they all met and churned together. Deals were cut. Investments were finalized. Appointments to high posts were determined. Perhaps even coups were plotted. This is where it all happened.

He checked into a mid-level room; probably booked by one of the Delhi boys. Nothing too ostentatious—he was a Canadian businessman, not an Arab sheikh. But not the cheapest one either. The optics around the story were as important as the story itself. He didn't waste much time. He gave a generous tip to the bellhop and asked for directions to the bar, while politely requesting for his luggage to be taken up.

For an Islamic country, the bar is rather full, he mused to himself. And it was only the afternoon. He picked a stool and a well-groomed bartender immediately attended to him.

'Sir, what can I get you?'

'Long flight, buddy. Do you have a Labatt Blue or a Molson?'

The bartender was apologetic. 'Sorry, sir, we don't keep Canadian beer. If you fancy North American fare, I could get you a Budweiser.'

Chang shook his head. 'Hell, no. I would rather have horsepiss. What else you got?'

'Sir, amongst the Chinese guests, Heineken and Tsingtao are popular.'

'But I am not just Chinese. I am Chinese Canadian. Anyway, tell you what...' Chang leaned in and slipped a 1000 rupee note to the bartender. 'I trust your judgment...get me what you would have.'

The bartender pocketed the cash and promptly got Chang a local brew—Murree. Chang took a sip and was genuinely impressed. It was a nice strong brew—once again, something he had not expected in an Islamic nation.

He slipped another 500 to the bartender. 'Good choice. Now what's your name?'

'Aslam, sir.'

'Aslam, you seem like a guy who knows his stuff. You must be keeping your eyes and ears open around the bar?'

'It's part of my job, sir.'

'Of course it is. I am here to explore the possibility of investing a considerable amount of money. I hear Chinese people are making fortunes here because of the CPEC. But I don't know where to begin. Could you put me in touch with someone who could get me in the thick of things quickly? I promise you a significantly heftier tip.'

'Sir, I think you have just arrived. You might be jet lagged. I suggest you take a short nap and come back to the bar later in the evening. I shall have just the right person.'

'Thanks, Aslam. Lovely beer, by the way.' He quickly finished the rest of the pint. *Now wait in the room, while Aslam taps into his network*, he thought. Espionage was as much about patience as it was about action.

Starbucks, Mumbai, India

Trevor was on time. It was an American trait which was never really appreciated by Indians who believed some leeway was always kosher. But unsurprisingly, given the circumstance, Aditi was already seated. She waved at him. He acknowledged the wave and walked towards the lounge chair.

Starbucks was one of the crown jewels of Pax Americana. A little bit of America in every corner of the world. You might get a sushi at the Starbucks in Tokyo and a samosa at the Starbucks in Mumbai, but the frappuccino remained the same. The interiors were similarly designed. Heck, they probably sourced the furniture from the same vendor. It made him proud.

Even as he pulled the couch to sit, he said, 'First and foremost, Aditi, on behalf of MindCorp, allow me to express...'

She held up her hand. 'Spare me the fake niceties. Where is he?'

'He was kidnapped, Aditi. We don't know. It's unprecedented. We are working with the local law enforcement.'

'*Local law enforcement?* You make them sound so professional. They are a bunch of inept, lazy buffoons and you know it.'

'What would you have me do?'

She folded her hands and reclined. 'You tell me, Trevor, what can you do?'

Trevor scratched his stubble. 'We will obviously continue to provide full salary and benefits to you till this issue is resolved. Additionally, if you require any counselling or monetary assistance, we would be more than happy to provide it.'

'That's bullshit. I need my husband, not a shrink. He was your employee.' She quickly corrected herself. 'He is your own employee! Man up and take some responsibility.'

Trevor said, 'I know you think it is all business for us. But I consider Udai to be a friend. Always have. And I shall do anything within my power to bring him back.'

'Why don't you get American cops involved?'

Trevor cracked a smile and shook his head. 'You've seen too many Hollywood movies. Should I just get *Starsky and Hutch?* The crime has been committed on Indian soil. It is their jurisdiction. And can you really see an American cop being able to work in such an environment?'

Aditi bit her lip. 'That's an excuse. Not a solution.'

Trevor hesitated. 'I will contact the American Consulate here in Mumbai, and even the embassy in New Delhi. I will see if they know something. But it might not be through official channels. And if I am able to find anything out, you must not leak it. We work with the Trade division guys and I will see if someone has heard something. Ok?'

Aditi nodded.

Trevor said, 'Now I shall go place the order. What would you like?'

Karachi, Pakistan

Watson walked into the room, with a smile plastered on his ready-to-be-punched face. 'Good news, Udai! We are getting out of here.'

'Thank God.'

'Or you could just thank me. Anyway, do you watch cricket?'

Udai frowned, as if asking himself, *who doesn't?*

Watson threw a plastic bag towards Udai. He opened it. In it was what looked like a soiled cricket uniform. 'What is this?'

'Just wear it and play along.'

'But the clothes are soiled.'

'That's by design.'

Udai put on the bright green uniform of 'Karachi Kings'; though unfamiliar with the team's name, he did not doubt its existence. There were a lot of T20 leagues these days. At the back, the name said 'Akram'. *Not bad*, thought Udai.

Udai asked, 'You are transporting me as a member of a cricket team?'

'Just put on the uniform.' Udai did as directed, still trying to figure out what was happening.

When he turned around, he saw a syringe in Watson's hand. A plethora of thoughts crossed his mind in an instant, even as Watson plunged the syringe into his neck. *This is it. They will kill me, transport my body, and extract the information. What a stupid way to die...*

Makeshift Police Office, Mumbai

Mayank could not help but notice, even as a woman grieving her kidnapped husband, Aditi turned a few heads. *How typical of people*, he thought. *In fact, it was easy to assume a beautiful lady crying as 'a damsel in distress'. Another stereotype.*

He wasn't a PR kind of guy. Even after the higher-ups in New Delhi pretty much forced his hand, Mayank had been reluctant to meet the wife. The only silver lining was that he could potentially get a better handle on the man kidnapped—Udai Sodha.

As Aditi seated herself across the table, he cleared some of the clutter on his desk. Both seemed to wait for the other to start the conversation. *It almost feels like a forced arranged marriage meeting*, mused Mayank. And then quickly realized that in many ways, it was. He bit the bullet.

'Mrs Sodha, I realize this isn't easy for you...'

She quipped, 'Please do away with the niceties, Mr Bose. I have had enough of such conversations offering all sorts of emotional support, backed by appropriate and politically correct words.'

Mayank let out a deep breath. 'That's absolutely fine with me, Mrs Sodha. To be honest, I am not very good at it.'

'Good. Can we get straight to the point? Where is Udai?'

Mayank offered a sheepish smile. 'I don't know. To be honest, I didn't even want to take this meeting, but apparently some people from the American Embassy in New Delhi have made a few calls to the Ministry of External Affairs. An important American employee, who is an Indian citizen, has been kidnapped. As the officer in charge, I have been asked to meet you. So here I am, doing this because of the Americans. So tell me, what can I do?'

Aditi stood up, picked up a paperweight from the table, and flung it at one of the window panes. As the glass shattered, Mayank got up from his chair. 'Lady, seriously—what the...'

'Oh, shut the fuck up, Bose. He is an Indian citizen. Shouldn't the Indians be updating me? The Americans don't need to tell you that, do they? I have gone to various police stations since my husband went missing. No one files an FIR. No one tells me the status of my husband. Is he dead, or alive? I am being shuttled from one office to the other. Finally, the Americans help a little, and you sit here comfortably in this little suite of yours and act as if you are doing me a favour?'

'I didn't mean it that way...'

'Sure you did. We are taxpaying, responsible citizens. You better give me some answers. You are the first officer whose name was given to me. If I don't get any answers, I am going to the press and giving them your name. You can tell them about your feelings about the Americans. We will see how that pans out.'

Mayank felt his cheeks flush. 'Ok, ok. You are right. I apologize. I should have put myself in your shoes. Let's just start afresh.'

'Yes, that sounds better, Mr Bose.'

Gesturing with his hand, Mayank made a circle in the air while saying, 'This entire office has been created for what has happened to your husband. Trust me, he is on a very high priority list for us. I do not wish to divulge secrets, which are forbidden under the Official Secrets Act (India). But what I can tell you is that your husband, Udai, has inside his mind the memories of a very important person.'

'Worth a lot of money?'

'It would have been a case for the Economic Offences Wing, if it was just about money, Mrs Sodha. I can't even imagine how invaluable the information your husband holds is. Not just to India, but also her enemies. Which is why, there are people not just in India, but even outside, who are trying to figure out what happened to Udai. There is no phone trace. There are no smoking guns. Whoever has kidnapped him, not only has a pretty good head start, but is also very bloody good.'

'So what are the chances of getting him back?'

'This is not a routine kidnapping, Mrs Sodha. I can't give you a figure.' He jotted down a number on a post-it. 'This is my personal number... Save it. Give me a missed call, so I can save yours. You can contact me anytime; I will be available 24x7. And as soon as I have any kind of lead, I shall contact you.'

Mayank thought that he heard a faint crack in her voice, as she said, 'Ok. Fair enough. But please do something.'

'Trust me. We are doing all we can. Now, if I may ask a few questions. What can you tell me about your husband? I have all his educational and professional details; his qualifications are very, very impressive. I have got them from MindCorp. But what kind of a person is he? Tell me something about him that his curriculum vitae doesn't say.' He gestured toward the empty chair.

Aditi sighed and sat down.

Serena Hotel, Islamabad, Pakistan

The bar was significantly more crowded as Chang walked in after a much deserved nap. As his eyes darted around the counter, he noticed a hand aloft. Aslam seemed to have a genuine smile on his face; not a typical hospitality smile.

Chang walked towards him. 'Hi, Aslam.'

'Good evening, sir.'

'Do you have something for me?'

'It is fairly crowded in here, so I've gotten a table ready for you by the pool. Someone important is waiting for you.'

Chang nodded. 'Thanks.' He opened his wallet and handed Aslam Rs 5000. *Courtesy of the Government of India,* he mused. 'Which way to the pool?'

'You won't be needing directions.'

'As in?'

'Well, sir, as soon as you step out of the bar, someone will be escorting you. I am afraid, they might frisk you.'

'Frisk me?'

'They just want to make sure that you are not wearing any listening device or carrying a weapon.'

Chang smiled. 'I am not used to this cloak-and-dagger routine. I am a businessman, not Jason Bourne.'

'Who is Jason Bourne?'

'He is like James Bond, only American.'

'Oh no, sir. You are definitely not James Bond.'

Chang laughed. As expected, he was met by a suited man right at the entrance of the bar. He ran a metal detector over Chang, and once satisfied, escorted him to the pool area on the upper level.

There was a sign outside: 'Pool shut for maintenance.'

Chang asked his escort, 'Maybe we are at the wrong pool. There are two, isn't it?'

The escort replied, 'It has been shut for your meeting. Let's go in.'

Chang was a bit anxious now. He bit his lip; tried to regain his composure. Whoever this was, Chang had to feign ignorance.

It was hard to do so once Chang realized who he was meeting. Waiting for him, dressed in full military regalia, was General Ahmed. Chang could not feign ignorance; he did not even try. This man's face was everywhere.

The General cheerfully said, 'You seemed surprised, Mr Chang.'

'Who wouldn't be? I was expecting a bureaucrat or a businessman. Not the most powerful man in Pakistan.'

The General smiled. 'Not really. Many would say the most powerful man in Pakistan sits in the Chinese embassy.'

'It's still your country though.'

'Of course, it is. And I am sorry about the frisking and the pat down. Just routine, you see.'

'No, not at all. No problem. Aslam has really outdone my expectations. I am glad to meet you.'

The General offered Chang one of the chilled Murree cans from an ice bucket. 'Aslam is the bartender downstairs?'

'Yes.'

The General popped a beer can for himself as well. 'Islamabad is a small town, Mr Chang. Word travels fast.'

'And what word would that be?'

'Aslam got in touch with someone. That got the ball rolling. While you were in your room, a lot of research was done on you. You represent the interests of Mapleton Infrastructure, headquartered in Alberta.'

Part of the plan to give me a cover. 'Yes, that's correct.'

'What is interesting is your company's assets. Yours is one of the 10 largest firms in Canada with a revenue which a country would be proud of.'

Great. Some overzealous IT guy in the Hyderabad office had done this. Like in Telugu films, the IT guy from Hyderabad had to exaggerate everything. 'Yes, it's not something we advertise. But if you dig into the public records, one can't really deny it.'

'So tell me, what brings you here? And how can we help you?'

'Well. You know who I represent. China has a lot of money. But that money has to go through a rather tedious state sanctioned process, if we are investing from mainland China.'

'But...?'

But a lot of Chinese money is in Canada. Away from the prying eyes of the Communist Party. And you would be surprised how much of that is from actual members of the politburo. Let's say, we have deep, deep pockets. And we too would like to profit from CPEC. Why should only those handpicked by the government be allowed to do so?'

The General was all smiles. Chang thought, *he might as well be wearing contact lenses with $ signs on them.* 'I couldn't agree more, Mr Chang. Tell me, what can I do?'

'In one word, "contracts". Contracts to build bridges, roads, housing colonies, and laying of railways. You need to show to the Pakistani people, and indeed the world, including institutions like the IMF that you are not bowing to the diktat of China by giving contracts only to state-run Chinese companies.'

The General scratched his beard and made a non-committal 'Hmm' sound.

'You give us the contracts and you win domestic audience by standing up to the Chinese. Chinese state-run firms require to hire mostly Chinese nationals. We don't do that; we will give sub-contracts to Pakistani firms owned by you or your friends. They can in turn hire locals. Foreign institutions and governments are happy that it is not China which is the only one milking the cow. And the best of all—the Chinese would be fine because, at the end of the day, it is the money of some very powerful people in China. And of course, there would be additional financial benefits for you.'

'I am sure. But why should I believe you?'

Chang considered for a moment. He removed his cell phone. 'How about I transfer $100,000 into your account right now to show how serious I am? No strings attached. Give me a bank number anywhere in the world and you will have the funds in, under a minute.'

The General picked up the gauntlet and gave him an account number to a bank in the Caribbean. Chang did not flinch either, but someone in New Delhi was going to be very upset. More than the fury, Chang dreaded the number of forms they would make him fill out, when he would get back. He transferred the amount.

The General immediately got an e-mail confirming the transfer. 'Ok, Mr Chang, you now have my unfettered and undivided attention. I would be happy to go into business with you.'

Chang took a sip of his beer and held up his pint. 'But there is something.'

'Tell me.'

'Well, actually, there are two concerns.'

The General was patient. 'I shall try and address them both then, Mr Chang.'

'First one: While we are willing to take certain risks, it would be foolish not to mitigate those risks through verification. We are particularly concerned in projects which will be constructed in what Pakistanis call "Azad Kashmir" and Indians consider "Pak-occupied Kashmir". Given the recent terror attacks in India, what is your assessment?'

The General deadpanned, 'My assessment about what?'

'Will there be war? Or any military action? Or anything that would put our investments in jeopardy—either now, or in the immediate future? I am not a political man, but I represent the interests of your potential investors.'

The General's face was impassive. 'I can't predict what the Indians will do. I am not a soothsayer.'

'Ah—a military man as well as a diplomat. Well, I shall be more direct, General.' *Ballsy. Risky. Suicidal.* A lot of adjectives crossed Chang's mind. 'Were you, or any Pakistanis in any way involved in the recent terror attacks in India? I need as much information as you have. We need clarity. All of us together are going to make a lot of money here. You understand my point?'

The General leaned back on his chair. He removed a pack of Marlboros and lit one with a Zippo. Chang could see what he was doing. *Weighing the odds. Potentially millions of dollars,*

Canadian citizenship for kith and kin, and a nice retirement versus classified information. Chang waited, not saying a word. Finally, the General said, 'Fine. But what I say is for your ears only. If it reaches your ambassador, the press, or anyone, if you are in Pakistan, you will not leave this country alive. If you are already out of Pakistan, be prepared to look over your shoulder for the rest of your life and, of course, we will never do business again. Is that clear?'

'The terms seem very fair to me, General.' *The mighty dollar always wins.*

The General stubbed his cigarette in the ashtray and leaned in once again, lowering his tone. 'The Pakistani Army and our Intelligence agencies had nothing to do with this attack. Neither serving, nor retired.'

Chang helped him along, 'But...'

The General let out a deep breath. 'Elements within Pakistan were tapped. These are associations who have enjoyed state and military patronage, but now have completely gone rogue. Money was wired in to them with exact plans. They were basically the mules who carried it out.'

'Money was wired to them from where?'

The General replied, 'The money came in from an account in the Cayman Islands. From there, it went to Dubai. From there, it was transferred to three different organizations in Pakistan. Each was contracted to carry out an operation in India. But that's not it.'

Chang continued chipping away. 'What do you mean?'

'The problem is that they were just too well coordinated. It wasn't like 26/11 in Mumbai, where a bunch of gunmen landed in a boat and just went around shooting people. This was coordinated like a bloody satellite launch.'

Chang completed what was left unsaid. 'Which means that they had a lot of local support. You can't coordinate this without local help.'

'Undoubtedly. Which is why, if the Indians do press us too much, through unofficial channels we will give them the financial smoking gun. This will lead them to Dubai and the Caymans. I assure you, Mr Chang, we *will* diffuse it with the Indians. We are not going to extradite anyone to India—that would be political suicide. But we will hand them enough information to calm them down.'

'General, I obviously believe you. But I also need to verify this information from independent sources of ours in the Caymans, maybe even in Dubai.'

The General raised his eyebrows. He didn't see that coming. 'That would be a bit much.'

Chang shrugged his shoulders. 'Everything has a price, General. I intend to keep my end of the bargain. This stays between us. I just need to verify that the transfer took place. For this, I am happy to transfer another $100,000 to your account.'

The General frowned. 'You must think we would do anything for money.'

'Most people do, isn't it?'

'Yeah. I guess so, Mr Chang. You will have the bank account details within the hour. You had another question for me?'

'Yes, the second point is about the deposed Prime Minister Khan.'

'What about him? Don't get all sentimental about him. I was the one who put him on that pedestal in the first place.'

'Honestly, I couldn't care less. He was deposed in a coup. He is fairly popular among the people. Do you see him playing some kind of role or doing anything that would bring him back to power? Because if he comes back, rest assured, he will scrap all the business deals we strike.'

The General vigorously shook his head. 'There is absolutely no chance.'

'Why is that?'

'Firstly, though in the past people have come back, now no one would want to go up against China. Earlier coups were domestic. China presents a new variable in the equation. And secondly, to save his neck, Khan sought refuge in India. We didn't expect that, but it is political suicide. His popularity has already waned, and through sustained propaganda, it will wane a lot more. He is not coming back. No chance.'

Chang nodded his head. 'Fair enough, General Ahmed. This is quite convincing.'

The General got up. Chang followed suit and extended his arm out. 'And you shall have the amount transferred as soon as I get that information about the bank accounts. May this be a strong and fruitful partnership.'

Over the Arabian Sea

Udai found himself mumbling. *I am dying. I am floating. What's that sound?* He opened his eyes.

He saw a silhouette. *God? No…it was that bastard Watson.*

'Udai, my man you are as strong as a horse. The effects were not supposed to wear off so fast.'

'Where am I, Watson?'

'You are in an air ambulance. You remember the cricket uniform?'

His mind was a bit clearer now. 'Yes, of course.'

'Well. That was your cover. You are an injured cricketer named "Taufiq Akram". Whilst batting, a bouncer hit your head and it is a life-threatening emergency. So we are taking you to Dubai for treatment.'

'And how stringent is the immigration going to be in the case of a life-threatening injury to a sportsman being transported by air ambulance?'

'Exactly. So continue your role as our star batsman. Immigration will be a breeze even in Dubai and we will take you straight to the Dubai Health City.'

'Which also houses MindCorp.'

Watson smiled. 'Tell me, you are impressed.'

Istanbul, Turkey

Chang did not need an Uber when he left the Serena to go to the airport. The General had provided him with a plush sedan for his flight back to Toronto via Istanbul.

Of course, despite his boarding pass in hand, Chang had no intention of flying to Canada.

He walked to a different boarding gate and flashed a different e-boarding pass on his cell phone. This time he wasn't travelling under the name 'Chang'. If the Pakistanis were keeping a tab, that would raise a red flag.

The lady at the boarding gate saw his boarding pass and double checked it with the Nepali passport to verify the name. 'Welcome on board Nepal Airways. Have a safe flight to Kathmandu, Mr Shakya.'

From Tribhuvan International Airport, he would board an Indigo flight to Mumbai under the same Nepali identity. Despite saddling him with millions in Canada, they had expectedly booked him on cattle class on the two legs. *When they find out how much I've had to bribe General Ahmed, next time they might just send me in the cargo hold.*

New Delhi, India

General Rodrigues waited patiently in the lobby with Lt General Burman. 'You know, Burman, we are probably the only country which threw off the colonial yoke, but has never had a coup—military or civilian.'

'Yes, that's true. Over 50 countries in Asia and Africa must have achieved their freedom within a decade of us. It's something to be proud of, no?'

'No, that's my point. Sometimes, when I am summarily summoned to answer these civilians, I wonder why.'

'I hope you are joking.'

'Of course I am, Burman. Lighten up.'

A peon came and said, 'Madam will see you now.'

As they entered the Defence Minister's office, they saw that Mishra was already there in his trademark attire, with the pens firmly in place. 'Madam, you called us?' ventured Burman.

'Gentlemen, please sit. And tell me, what's the latest on the assassination? We can't keep the press at bay. I have a press conference later this evening. I don't want to be blindsided there. Is there anything in the public domain?'

Rodrigues said, 'Nothing from us. In fact, we are still in the throes of cracking the case.'

Mishra asked, 'How long will it take?'

Rodrigues said, 'We are trying to find this Sodha fellow. We have an entire team working on it. He is a walking time bomb. His presence will raise an alarm. We will send a team and exfiltrate him. We will do whatever it takes.'

The Minister said, 'Even from a dangerous, or non-friendly country?'

Burman said, 'All the MindCorp offices are in friendly countries—mostly in countries, which are staunch American allies. So he is not going to be in Karachi or Pyongyang for sure.'

Mishra said, 'Speaking of Americans, there is that McGregor fellow who wants to meet you.'

The Minister nodded her head and looked at Mishra. Returning the glance, Mishra too started nodding his head, even as Rodrigues rolled his eyes. *Americans.*

Mumbai, India

Rao and Chang walked towards Mayank. Rao said, 'Sir, this is Chang.'

'No shit. Doesn't exactly look like a Subramanian. Who else could he possibly be?' He turned to Chang, accusingly pointing a finger at him—'Have you fucking lost your mind, Chang?'

Chang was taken aback. 'What? I haven't even given you a report yet.'

'Yeah, but I got a whole bunch of calls from New Delhi. Did you wire transfer 200,000 American dollars to some contact in the Caribbean?'

Chang was a little sheepish. 'Yes, I did.'

Mayank threw up his hands. 'Who do you think we are? The CIA? We don't have that kind of cash to burn. The guys in Delhi told me that my contact might have siphoned off the money himself and absconded. So your explanation better be good.'

'Wait till you hear it.'

'What is this? You're channelling your inner Hitchcock? Out with it!'

Without being invited to, Chang sat down. 'The money was transferred to the personal account of General Ahmed.'

'THE General Ahmed?'

'Yes.'

Mayank shook his head. 'You contacted the top ranking Pakistani General in 24 hours and got information out? New Delhi is more likely to believe the absconder theory.'

Chang threw up his hands. 'Honestly, I was shocked too. But Islamabad is a small town. It is just diplomats and power brokers. It's quite pretty too—lush and green, with wide roads.'

Mayank frowned. 'Did you also do a course in those 24 hours to become a Pakistani tour guide?'

Chang smiled. 'They really love the Chinese there. Well, at least the power brokers do, if not the common people.' Chang handed Mayank a pen drive. 'This has the report. And you need to verify a few account numbers. You trace them and we will get an idea of who is responsible for the terror attacks and maybe even who has got that Sodha fellow.'

Mayank gave the pen drive to Rao. 'Back it up and send the data in encrypted form to the Bangalore lab. Try and get the information as soon as possible.'

Chang asked, 'Should I head to New Delhi then?'

Mayank shook his head. 'I have requisitioned you. You are going to be here for a while; we might need you. Good work, Chang. I am very impressed. Find yourself a desk, while I go through your report. Rao must have uploaded it by now on the common drive.'

'And what should I do?'

Mayank winked at him. 'Play a game on your phone, or watch a movie for all I care. You have earned a break.'

Dubai, UAE

Watson was facing a nervous wreck of a manager at the MindCorp office in Dubai. The nameplate on the door said 'Anderson'—one of the many British expats in Dubai who got a fat salary for being white and speaking good English. Watson didn't care much for the lot.

Anderson said, 'You know, Udai is a MindCorp employee. You can't just bully me into submission.'

'Relax, Anderson. You process him, we take the memories out, you can keep him, and I will be out of your hair. You can say I forced your hand. You won't be lying—your wife and son are...well...our guests at the moment. Knowing how fragile your situation is, what will they do to you?'

'What do you mean?'

Watson explained. 'You save your family. You save your employee. All you lose is a hard drive. And you get a nice bonus cheque from us. How is this bad for you?' He continued, 'He is in a hospital in Health City under a false name. We can have him here in 10 minutes. I just want to make sure that we are clear on the process.'

Anderson sighed. 'Yes, you've mentioned it three times. We cut off all Internet access and switch off the CCTVs. We also turn over all cell phones to you. You will then bring him in. You will pay double the usual price. There will be no backup—you will straight away take the data on a hard disk. Once you are out of here, we are free to do as we please with Udai. And your men will leave my wife and son at The Mall of the Emirates.'

'Bingo.'

'I don't understand one thing. You take the data, but how will you read it? You need access to our neural network.'

'I have two words for you—Rosetta Stone.'

Anderson shook his head. 'No such thing exists. It is a myth.'

Watson walked towards Anderson and caressed his jacket. 'Do you think, we would not have thought this through unless we had a way to access the data? You are free to believe what you want. All I need you to do is to follow directions. Is that going to be a problem?'

'No, you can bring him in.'

'Let's start with the cell phones, wallets, and Internet access first.'

Anderson called all 17 employees to the conference room. One by one, everyone handed in their cellular phones. He then directed the IT technician to switch off Internet access as well as the CCTV.

Watson tapped the desk. 'Don't worry, this is a drill because of what happened in Mumbai. We are just seeing what can possibly go wrong.' He held up a bag. 'All your cell phones and wallets will be with me at all times. Don't worry about it at all.'

He turned to the IT technician. 'You should also delete all CCTV footage from today that is already recorded. Let this be a ghost day.'

One of the nurses shot her hand up and asked, 'But why?'

Watson said, 'We are trying to create the worst possible situation in light of what happened in Mumbai. Don't worry, specific questions of yours will be answered at the EoD exercise. We value your feedback.'

The employees murmured amongst themselves and a majority of them nodded.

Anderson said, 'Now resume your duties. We will be getting a subject for neural transfer soon. Get the OT ready.'

As the employees left the room, Watson gave Anderson a thumbs up sign.

Watson then sent a quick text. Within the next 10 minutes, an ambulance from a nearby hospital entered into the parking lot of MindCorp and Udai was lowered on a wheelchair. He looked at the sign of MindCorp and breathed a sigh of relief. *Finally.*

Watson tipped the ambulance personnel and decided to personally wheel Udai in. 'Buddy, we made it. Just a few more hours and you will be free.' Udai nodded.

As directed by Anderson, the medical support staff shifted Udai to a stretcher and led him straight to the OT. Both Anderson as well as Watson accompanied them inside.

As soon as Udai was plugged into the neural network, the system recognized him. The doctor heading the team appeared a little confused, 'If this is the guy kidnapped from Mumbai...'

Watson shook his head and pulled his gun out. 'Then I am afraid, I am the kidnapper. Now quickly complete the process, backup the data from the deceased guy on a hard drive, and give it to me. I am sure Udai will survive.'

The doctor looked at Anderson with an accusatory look. The manager couldn't muster the courage to look at his crew in the eye. Watson waved the gun once again. 'I really don't want to use this. I know you all are confused. Just do as told and nothing will happen to you lot.' He then specifically instructed the doctor, 'Just get on it with it, Doc.'

The doctor nodded assent. 'Very well.'

Udai was put under anaesthesia. Given his state, he hardly seemed to notice going under.

The doctor said, 'We have to bring his blood pressure and heart rate under control. He is also running a temperature, which is not ideal.'

Watson asked, 'How much time?'

The doctor said, 'A couple of hours—maybe a little more.'

Watson said, 'That's fine.' As the doctor turned to his staff, Watson beckoned him once again. 'Err, Doctor. If it boils down to saving the data, or saving Udai, I love Udai very much, but you will have to save the data. Ok?'

Mumbai, India

Mayank gave Chang a sheet of paper. It had all sorts of financial information on it. Chang's frown showed that accounting was not his favourite subject. 'Am I supposed to understand this?'

Mayank replied, 'Yes. Ideally, you should. But let me give you a gist.' He took the paper from Chang's hand. 'This paper shows the money trail that General Ahmed was referring to.'

'And does it tell us anything?'

'It tells us that a total of 11 banking institutions across the Caribbean from Antigua to Bermuda, to Belize, to Nevis were used. Money was routed and rerouted; currency was exchanged from Dollar or Euro, and back. Each of these accounts is protected by a variety of local banking laws there. And even then, there are layers of shell companies.'

'So all the information that I got from Ahmed is essentially useless?'

'Not quite, look here.' Mayank showed him a bunch of numbers which stood out in red.

'Is the colour significant?'

Mayank looked at him as if Chang was an idiot. But then again, not everyone had been trained in the financial aspects of intelligence. 'Because of Pakistan's history with terror financing, the State of Pakistan has for years been on the FATF grey list.'

'Yes, I do remember reading about that.'

Mayank continued. 'Black list is pretty bad. Grey list is only slightly better. Basically, it means that money coming into Pakistan is highly regulated by international agencies and only a few banks are allowed to operate. It basically stifles them and makes it rather tedious to transfer funds into Pakistan. Only a few banks are allowed to do so. Are you with me?'

'Yes, so far.'

'So Caribbean banks can't transfer money straight to Pakistan. All those smokescreens they put up don't help them. What these red numbers tell us is that from all these banks, only one particular bank was used as a final funnel to transfer the money to Pakistan.'

'Which one?'

'From the banking codes, we can see that it is one branch of one bank. In fact, that bank has only one branch; it's so bloody nondescript. The name of the bank is Al-Fatah Bank, in Dubai. Caters almost exclusively to Pakistani lower income expats for transferring their hard-earned Middle Eastern labour wages back home to Pakistan.'

Chang interjected—'And because there are so many Pakistanis in UAE and the surrounding Arab states, a spike in transfer from Al-Fatah Bank to Pakistani banks would not raise FATF eyebrows.'

Mayank winked at him. 'You are getting good at this! Yes, a minor spike would not really be noticed by FATF, or by any other agency. Workers could have received bonuses that month or something, perhaps a 10–15 per cent spike.'

'That's pretty smart. But what do we do now?'

Mayank gave him an 'I can't believe I have to answer that' look. 'Chang, we now go to Dubai.'

MindCorp Dubai

The doctor turned to Watson. 'The procedure is complete. We are waking Udai up.'

Watson nodded. 'Ok. And what about the data?'

'It is really very large. You want it on a hard drive—it would take several hard drives to move the data into and several hours. The problem is...'

Watson interjected, 'You don't need to prove to me that you are a geek, Doctor. I am sold already. Just tell me, how much data can you fit into one hard drive—the largest one available?'

The doctor scratched his head. 'Some years have better memories than others…'

Watson said, 'I am sure they do. And I am sure he had wonderful memories of his honeymoon. As much as I would love to see them, they really are not a priority.'

The doctor shrugged, 'It's just difficult to say…'

Watson took out the gun. 'For fuck's sake. Doctor, just give me a ballpark figure.'

Anderson interjected, 'Can you please just put away the gun. We have all cooperated, haven't we?'

The doctor took a couple steps back and spilled some tools on the floor. 'Ok. Ok. Maybe about 7–10 years. We can use indexing algorithms to get memory data from specific years.'

Watson rolled his eyes. 'There you go. That's more than enough. I am giving you a 7–8 year time frame; backup the data between 1996 and 2003, and hand it to me.' Watson put the gun away. Out of the corner of his eye, he saw some movement. Udai was finally waking up. 'Get up Udai. The worst is over.'

A few minutes later, the doctor handed him a hard drive. 'That's about five teraflops. I could compress the quality of the memories and you will have about 10–11 years, from 1994 to 2004.'

Watson said, 'That's excellent. Now delete all the data from your servers, hard drive, etc. I don't even want a single digital footprint.'

Anderson gestured to the guy manning the computer who did as directed. 'Done. All data has been deleted from MindCorp servers.'

'Excellent!' said Watson, as he put the drive in a padded case and kept it in one of his pockets.

As soon as he did, he felt a jarring pain in his head. He turned around and saw Udai; his eyes were red and movement unsteady. Yet he was still quick enough to land another blow on Watson's head with his bare knuckles. *Boy, the man packed a punch,* thought Watson as he felt his knees buckle.

As Watson fell on the floor, Udai reached into Watson's pockets and grabbed the gun. 'You are probably still groggy, Udai. You mustn't...'

Udai hit Watson's temple with the butt of the gun. 'Shut up, fuckface. You have given me enough grief. Give me the hard drive.'

Still reeling from the blow Watson said, 'You know, I can't do that.'

Udai didn't flinch. He looked at the gun, put the safety off and shot Watson in the foot. Watson yelled in pain. 'Seriously?'

'Give me the bloody hard drive, Watson.'

Watson handed him the padded case. Udai quickly unzipped it and checked it.

Anderson spoke, 'Excellent job, Udai. Allow me to introduce...'

Udai pointed the gun at him as well. 'Shut up. I don't know who is involved with these fuckers and who is not. All I see is that the cameras are off and you are doing this Watson's bidding.' As he said it, he kicked Watson in the gunshot wound. Ignoring his cries, Udai continued, 'Who is the anaesthetist here?'

One of the crew lifted her hand. Udai looked at the name tag—it had a Greek sounding name. 'Ms Dukas, I want you to put each of these people under. Let's start with Watson here.'

Anderson once again tried to speak, 'May I...'

'I had no problems shooting Watson. So I would not have any problems shooting you. So keep your mouth shut.' He saw Watson writhing in pain. *How the tables had turned.* 'Oh, Watson. Just bear the pain,' he chided. 'Ms Dukas, go ahead.' She injected him.

Udai read the doctor's name tag and said, 'Now, it's the turn of Mr Anderson.' The entire crew was put under anaesthesia.

Udai asked, 'How long will they be under?'

'At least 2 hours each. Please, I knew nothing...'

Udai shook his head. 'I know. I am sure most of you don't know anything. But I can't waste any time trying to figure that out. I don't know who in our company has or hasn't sold out and who isn't. So I am going to take this hard drive and leave. I can take no chances. So I will gag you and tie you to that chair.' She was pleading with her eyes. Udai felt sorry for her. He winced and continued. 'It will just be a couple of hours. Someone will get up and untie you. I truly am sorry about this.'

He bound her to the chair and gagged her with a scarf. He then looked for the wallets of those under. After checking two people and not finding anything on them, he looked at Dukas.

With her eyes she pointed towards a bag in the corner. Udai opened it and saw that the bag contained the cell phones and wallets of all the personnel. He quickly transferred all the cash into one wallet and grabbed three of the cell phones. He switched them on and put them in airplane mode. He mouthed a thanks and gave a thumbs up sign to Dukas. He removed his green gown. He then put on a surgical mask and a pair of gloves, and removed Watson's clothes and put them on. He found a lab coat and put that on as well.

Giving one final kick to the comatose naked body of Watson, he exited the operation theatre.

Both Mayank and Chang had been booked on separate flights. They couldn't risk to be seen together despite Chang's constant pleas that all Chinese looked the same to Indians and Pakistanis.

Given the plethora of flights from Mumbai to Dubai, this was not a problem. They arrived within 15 minutes of each other at the same terminal. They stood in separate emigration queues. And they finally took separate cabs to the same hotel. Even their rooms were on different floors.

After checking in, Chang kept his luggage and headed down to Mayank's floor. Mayank opened the minibar and handed Chang a bottle of water.

Mayank said, 'We first need to head to this bank. What I think we should do is...' His sentence was interrupted by his vibrating cell phone; it was still on silent mode. Lt General Burman's name flashed across the screen.

Mayank promptly answered, 'Yes, General?'

Mayank kept talking in a hushed voice. 'In Dubai...yes, sir... will do right away....Yes.' He hung up and looked at Chang.

Chang asked, 'Well? What happened now?'

Mayank replied, 'It seems all roads lead to Dubai.'

'What do you mean?'

'Maybe it's nothing. Trevor Davis from MindCorp, Mumbai, called their office in New Delhi. He has informed them that there seems to be some issue at the Dubai MindCorp.'

'What kind of issues?'

'That's the thing. It is pretty vague. Maybe it is nothing. Their systems are completely down and that has never happened. There are multiple fail-safes to prevent that. But Burman said we better go check it out.'

'What about the bank?'

'Yeah, we need to split up. You head to the bank and I will go check out what exactly is happening at MindCorp here.'

Even though it had only been a few days, the sense of relief that Udai felt was immense. The head was no longer throbbing. He was no longer kidnapped. The last few days had been surreal.

But a number of questions remained. *How do I get back to Mumbai? Why was the Pakistani ex-PM murdered? What's in that hard disk?* But the number one question in his mind was—*What the fuck is going on?*

He had a significant amount of cash. That was a bit of a silver lining. He hailed a cab and asked the Bangladeshi cabbie to take him to The Mall of the Emirates. Its sheer size was going to make it easy to get lost.

He was still dressed in Watson's clothes which were ill-fitting. He entered a Levi's store in the mall and changed into a t-shirt and a pair of jeans. He also bought a cap—always helpful to hide a face from CCTV cameras.

Next, he entered a Tim Hortons in the mall.

The kid behind the counter was cheerful. 'Yes, sir?'

'Just get me a cappuccino. Large, in skim milk.'

'Anything to eat, sir?'

Udai looked at the menu. It made him realize that he was quite hungry. He looked at Fusion Shawarma and afforded himself a smile. *Tim Hortons is selling shawarma! We indeed live in a surreal world.* 'I will have the shawarma.'

'Sure, sir. Will that be all?'

'Do you have the WiFi password?'

The kid gave him a scratch card. 'This has a password. It is valid for 30 mins. If you plan on staying longer, just come on up and I will give you another scratch card.'

Udai mouthed a thank you and took the scratch card.

He removed one of the three phones he had taken from the hospital. *No point going online on a cellular network, that would leave a digital trail*, he thought. He logged into the WiFi at the coffee shop and started reading the news from the time he was kidnapped.

He was surprised to read that the news did not even mention him. Only a small incident at MindCorp, Mumbai, had found a passing mention in some of the news outlets.

He then ran a Google search for Prime Minister Ishtiaq Khan. Again, the search showed results which shocked him. There was no mention of his death—everything had been kept under wraps—which was no mean achievement in this day and age. He downloaded the app and logged into his Skype account. He gestured to the kid working at the counter.

'Listen, buddy, do you have a debit or credit card?'

The boy nodded looking at Udai as if to say, *who doesn't?*

'I have just moved here and the bank takes a few days to issue a new debit card. I need to make a few calls back home to India. Can you load about 300 dirhams worth of credit and I shall happily give you 500 dirhams in cash. It's pretty urgent.'

Which teenager would refuse some extra cash? The boy shrugged and bought him the credits in exchange for the cash.

Udai dialled Aditi. She started crying as soon as she heard his voice. After a few seconds, she regained her composure and asked, 'Where are you?'

Udai ignored the question. 'Aditi, listen—why isn't my kidnapping in the news?'

'They said it was a matter of national importance. They said that you have some important information. They really made me run around. What a country…'

'Yeah, yeah, I know that. Now listen. I am trying to put the pieces together. I will call you again soon. Bye.'

Should I go to the Indian Consulate here? What if that is being watched by Watson's men? What if they don't let me in? I don't have any papers.

He checked his wallet. He counted the cash from the MindCorp employees. Udai gulped down his last sip of coffee as he mentally finalized his next course of action.

Manama, Bahrain

Fixer was in the Jacuzzi, when the alarm on his cell phone started blaring. Four hours—that was three strikes! It had been four hours since Watson had last checked in. He was supposed to check in every hour from Dubai. He may have missed it once because of inadvertent delays, but four hours was far too long. *Hope for the best, prepare for the worst.*

If Fixer was perturbed about this development, he did not show it. He was the best in the business, because he was always two steps ahead of the game, if not three. Whilst still in the pool, he inserted an IP address into the browser of his cell phone. A drone whirred in Dubai outside the MindCorp office. On 16x Rewind mode he started seeing the footage at the entrance—there was supposed to be no movement. In a few minutes he noticed that a man dressed as a doctor had stepped out of the office. His face wasn't clear. So Fixer ran the parameters of his height and weight. There was no doubt in his mind.

That Indian son of a bitch had somehow managed to escape, probably with the data.

Fixer opened a folder in one of his cloud accounts, and went through a document. He made some changes and sent it to a variety of news outlets across India, and the world, from an untraceable e-mail account through a VPN. *With every channel battling for TRPs and eyeballs, this should be a breeze,* he chuckled. *Fact checks were history.*

Within half an hour, every news channel worth its screeching anchor was trying to outdo the others with graphics: 'Burning Questions' and 'Breaking News'—all from unverified sources, of course.

Fixer tuned into the live feeds of one of the channels. The bombastic news anchor Hazarika on OurNation channel was going hammer and tongs at confused panelists who had come to discuss a completely different issue. *News in India deserves to have an entertainment tax.* Mr Hazarika, sweating profusely, kept raising the decibel metre.

'Gentlemen, if you are just joining us—this is breaking news—brought to you by your own channel. OurNation has in its possession a letter which states the former Prime Minister of Pakistan, Mr Khan, has been brutally assassinated in India. His alleged killer is a certain man by the name of "Udai Singh Sodha", who used to work in MindCorp, Mumbai. All this information had been kept hidden from you, my dear viewers, by our government. He has stolen the memories of Mr Khan and other vital national secrets, and is now holding our country to ransom. This absconding suspect is believed to be in the Middle East. Mr Sodha has spent some time in England where he may have been radicalized by Muslim or Khalistani extremists.'

Fixer laughed aloud at the last line. He hadn't even mentioned any such thing. It was all a product of the rather fertile imagination of Mr Hazarika.

'Government sources continue to dodge us, avoid our calls and are tight lipped. But dear viewer, your channel will dig up facts from the pits of hell, if it has to. Stay tuned...'

Fixer had set the bulls loose; he wondered what the bulls would do to all the china shops in the game...

Edgar Hoover Building, Washington DC, USA

The Vice President, and the Secretary of State, Upton, were huddled together in a meeting with the Deputy Director of CIA who was the de facto CIA chief since the firing of his boss. Emerson had always wanted the job, even coveted it. But this was quite possibly the worst of times to step into those shoes.

The Vice President asked, 'How accurate is the news about Prime Minister Ishtiaq Khan?'

Emerson said, 'Well, all the news channels say that the reports are being verified.'

The Vice President shot back, 'So is the CIA now going to wait for CNN to confirm what's going on?'

Emerson shook his head. 'The Indians would have issued a blanket statement almost immediately, if this report was false. They have gone into a huddle. And one of our sources in New Delhi said that there is definitely something to the rumours.'

Secretary Upton asked, 'Is there something in Khan's memories that would be a problem for us?'

Emerson sighed. 'Loads. Secret deals for drone strikes in civilian regions. In his first term, we negotiated for a base which allowed us aerial surveillance into China. We paid "blood money" for the release of some American aid workers who had been captured. We had drones flying over Iran which flew from Pakistan. We have had payoffs to various members of his family for all sorts of deals. We even got one of his opium-addicted kids into Harvard.'

The Vice President threw up his hands. 'We build airplanes and the bastards weaponize those and blow up the World Trade

Center. We build something revolutionary like MindCorp and the bastards find a way to weaponize that as well. POTUS and I are clear—let the idiots in Asia handle this, but keep an eye out. We here will blame the previous administration if something untoward comes out. But we need to keep ourselves abreast of what's going on; so send someone there who can help things along. Jumpstart the process for the Indians, if you will.'

The Islamabad Club, Islamabad, Pakistan

General Ahmed politely refused what he had seen as another summons from the Chinese Ambassador. The Chinese, desperate to get a handle on things, agreed to meet at the neutral Islamabad Club, another favourite of the diplomatic community in Islamabad.

Ambassador Huang knew that Ahmed had more respect for a man in uniform than a civilian, so he decided to let Colonel Lin take the initiative.

Lin asked, 'General, what do we know about the case of Mr Khan?'

The Pakistani shrugged. He was more interested in the whisky than in the conversation. 'Good riddance to bad rubbish. He was a thorn in our flesh. Shouldn't we be happy he is gone?'

Huang asked, 'Did you have anything to do with...'

Ahmed seemed genuinely hurt. 'You must think I am incredibly stupid. If he had remained a refugee in India, his support among Pakistani people would have waned. We would keep reminding them that he was always an Indian agent. Now that he is dead, his supporters will come up with all sorts of theories and make him a martyr.'

The Ambassador asked, 'What about the data, that is, his memories?'

Ahmed said, 'I bet they are filled with visits to every brothel in Lahore and Karachi. I honestly don't care. He might have had state secrets, but nothing too important. The civilian leadership here has always been on a need-to-know basis.'

Lin interjected, 'That makes sense. No skin off our nose.'

Ambassador Huang shook his head. 'No, no. That data might give us some insights into his relations with USA, with Britain. We must try to get it.'

Ahmed was taken aback. The Chinese never disagreed. At least not in front of him. He looked at Colonel Lin who himself wasn't very happy. At the end of the day, Huang was called 'Viceroy' for a reason. Ahmed said, 'I will see what I can do.'

Defence Ministry, New Delhi, India

Defence Minister Raman was livid. 'I don't understand. How did this information leave this circle? There has been a major breach.'

Mishra said, 'Madam, it is most unfortunate...'

The Defence Minister raised her hand. '*Chamchagiri band karo*. We have to issue some statement to the news channels. My spokespersons have all switched off their mobile phones. The opposition leaders are on every channel milking this moment to the hilt.'

She looked at General Rodrigues. He said, 'Madam, this is in the civilian domain. What statement you issue is entirely your prerogative. I've instructed the army spokesperson to state that all questions must be directed to the Defence Ministry.'

Mishra said, 'What sort of attitude is this?'

Rodrigues said, 'Governments come and go, Mishra. As do bureaucrats. The Indian Army can't favour the viewpoint of any one party. We will not get involved in your mudslinging games.'

Even as Mishra's face reddened, the Defence Minister said, 'What do you suggest, Mishra? General Rodrigues, you can give me a proper assessment as well.'

Rodrigues said, 'Issue a statement that Prime Minister Khan is dead. The boy, Sodha, is innocent and was kidnapped. And that we are doing our best to get him back. I suggest you share this with the opposition leader too, so that they tone down their rhetoric.'

Mishra said, 'What nonsense! We say the Pakistani Prime Minister under our care was assassinated? Then one man stole his memories and kidnapped this Sodha chap? And then you expect the opposition to remain quiet? Rodrigues, this is not how politics works.'

The Defence Minister said, 'Mishra is right. We will inform the spokespersons to confirm that Prime Minister Khan was assassinated. On Udai Sodha, we will say that we are pursuing all leads and the ministry would not like to comment on an ongoing investigation, but it is true that he has disappeared.'

Rodrigues said, 'I really don't think that's fair to the boy.'

Mishra even managed to sound wistful and sad. 'C'est la vie, Rodrigues. Life is never fair.'

Mall of the Emirates, Dubai, UAE

Udai was still in the mall, albeit in a different café. He didn't want to stick to the same WiFi hotspot. He felt the phone vibrate in his pocket. He was still not connected to any cellular network so it had to be his wife, probably messaging on Skype. The message was indeed from Aditi. Given her propensity for long messages, this was both cryptic and short. *First time for everything,* he mused. The message simply read: 'Check the news. Now.'

Following a wife's diktat was almost muscle memory for anyone who has been married for more than five years. He quickly scanned a news site. *Shit.* He then tried a couple more, and on every Indian news outlet, his face was flashed right at the top of the page. Every story was a variant of the same. Udai had allegedly murdered the former Prime Minister of Pakistan. He had bolted with memories of national importance. And, of course, thanks to the ingenuity of the bombastic Mr Hazarika he had allegedly hobnobbed with Khalistani and Pakistani terror cells in London. The government sources were neither confirming, nor denying anything about Mr Udai Singh Sodha. But they were happy to confirm that the former Prime Minister of Pakistan had left for his heavenly abode in an unnatural way. *They might as well draw a bullseye at the back of my head.*

He wondered if the shades and the baseball cap helped mask his identity, but it was no longer very safe to hang around in a crowded mall; it was only a matter of time before someone recognized him.

This was a problem. He didn't want to go on the grid by accessing a cell phone network, but he still needed access to the Internet. If public WiFi was not available, he was in a soup.

He looked for IP masking VPN apps. It was probably illegal in UAE, but considering they were pinning murder charges on him, he was willing to chance breaking some random local IT laws. He found an APK file for a software called 'Hide.Me' on a Russian website. *Trust the Russians to design something to hoodwink the authorities. After all, they had eons of experience,* thought Udai. He sideloaded Hide.Me on the cell phone after enabling the developer mode.

The app allowed him to choose a country, whose IP he could spoof. He chose the Democratic Republic of Congo. He then switched off the WiFi and went online on the network. Theoretically, if anyone traced him, it would show that he was browsing from the Congo. He didn't know if it would really work. He said a silent prayer and decided to exit the mall.

MindCorp, Dubai

Mayank was expecting to saunter in and ask a few questions. He didn't have any jurisdiction, so he would have to pose as a potential client. He didn't expect to see a whole bunch of police cars and ambulances right outside the premises; it seemed pretty chaotic.

He tried getting in but was stopped by a uniformed cop. The cop spoke English in a thick Arabic accent. 'Only authorized personnel or Emergency Medical Services.'

Mayank asked, 'Uh...can I speak to the man in-charge?'

'You *are* speaking to the man in-charge. Officer Abboud.' He held out his hand, 'And you are?'

Mayank took it. 'I am from an agency in India. I need to find out what happened here.'

'Which agency? Space agency?'

Mayank shook his head. The Arab continued, 'See, I can't let anyone in. You are not even telling me where you are from. Your embassy can request my government to give access.'

Just then Mayank heard an American accent. 'I'd wager he is from RAW. His name is Mayank Bose.'

Mayank turned around to see a man clearly not used to being in the desert. His cheeks were red despite his generously applied sunblock, which was now mixing with perspiration and rolling out of his pores. Alarmingly he was dressed in a suit, hardly the best attire for the weather. 'I am Andy McGregor.'

Mayank shook his hand. 'I'd wager you are from the CIA.'

McGregor smiled. 'Yeah, well, it's not a secret. I understand you want access to what happened here.'

'Yes, I do. How do you know my name?'

'Didn't I just say that I am from the CIA?' Mayank nodded and gave a wry smile. McGregor continued, 'Well, you can either go through the diplomatic channels. Maybe in a week or two, the government here might give you limited access, or I can give you full access right now.'

'I assume that you want something in exchange?'

McGregor clicked his tongue. 'Good old quid pro quo.'

Mayank asked, 'What do you want?'

McGregor replied, 'I want all the information you have about Sodha and I want to be kept in the loop about any development. Additionally, if you get any information from Mr Sodha that is inimical to American interests, you will let me know ASAP.'

Mayank laughed. 'I know we are in Arabia. But do I look like a fucking genie? You want all that information in exchange for access to one building?'

'As you know, we have unfettered access to every department in the UAE. In addition, I can tell you that the local police have captured the very man who most likely kidnapped Mr Sodha and you might just get to speak to him.'

Mayank considered, 'I shall have to check with New Delhi.'

McGregor shook his head. 'Don't bother. I just came from there. They are still sitting on the fence and will tell you to do the same. They are considering political and bureaucratic angles. Intelligence work is done on the basis of instant decisions.' He paused. 'But it is still your call.'

Mayank wondered if he should confer with Chang. He decided against it and said resolvedly, 'Fine, McGregor, but all of this will be off-the-record.'

'Certainly. We are on the same team here.' McGregor nodded to the Arab cop who grudgingly let the Indian in along with the American.

As they walked in, McGregor briefed him on what happened.

Mayank asked, 'So, is Udai in Dubai?'

McGregor didn't seem sure. 'He was. A few hours ago. It's pretty complicated as I have been explaining to the local force here. He hasn't entered on his own passport. He hasn't technically committed a crime that has been reported. A doctor here claims that he stole a hard drive, but that's hardly the kind of crime which would make them deploy their snipers. So someone from Langley is speaking to someone here, and soon the wheels will be in motion. We can jumpstart it much quicker than New Delhi.'

Mayank admitted, 'I don't doubt that. What I can tell you about Udai is that he is very smart and physically very fit. He doesn't have any military training or tactical nous, but with the IQ and fitness he has, he must have good survival skills. You know, the MindCorp employees are required to take up some form of martial arts.'

'Really?'

Mayank continued, 'Yes, and Udai has taken up Krav Maga—one of the toughest of the lot, perfected by the Israelis. We spoke to his coach in India. He said that the guy is impressive and dedicated. But we will come to all that. What about the guy who was caught here?'

McGregor replied, 'He was going by the name Watson. But that's not his real name.'

'Then what is?'

McGregor continued. 'His real name is Jean Pierre Ahmed. He is half French and half Pakistani—his mother is French. He has conveniently dropped "Ahmed" and has chosen "Pascal" as his last name. Obviously, he has a French passport. He did briefly attend an Islamic seminary in Lyon. This is why he is in our database. But he was not radicalized, nor is he a part of any Jehadi network. Well educated, he speaks multiple languages fluently. The local police want to arrest him. I have requested them to keep him here for a while, so that I can speak to him. But I am a pen pusher. Would you like to speak to him, while I watch? You seem like more of a field agent.'

'And you trust me?'

'I will be watching, as I said. And yeah, I trust you. I've read your file, Mr Bose. We are the CI fucking A. You trust me, I trust you.' He pointed to a door. 'You ready?'

Mayank opened it and entered as McGregor followed him in. Mayank felt a chill; they had clearly set the temperature at the lowest possible level. They had also not bothered to clothe Watson in anything except for a towel. He was shivering intermittently, sitting on a metal chair in the centre of the room. He looked at the two men and did not bother to offer an expression; he just had a stoic look.

Mayank looked once at McGregor before saying. 'So we know your legal name is Jean Pierre Pascal. Earlier it was Jean Pierre Ahmed. Now, if we run some recognition software, we will place you in India at MindCorp, Mumbai, bringing in Prime Minister Khan. You broke some local laws in Dubai as well. I am assuming that the Emiratis will try you for that and you will face some jail time here too.'

Pascal shrugged. 'I was Sinha in India, and then Watson. I kind of liked that name. Feels odd to be called Pascal.'

Mayank moved closer. 'Hmm. If you go to an Arab prison, some sheikh might take a fancy to you and make you Princess

Jasmine. How's that for a new name?' Pascal did not respond. Mayank continued, 'Anyway Pascal, the point is that your goose is cooked. Now my American friend here has some serious pull in the local government. That's why an Indian is interrogating you. So I suggest you cooperate with us and we can perhaps help you with the charges here.'

'Help me with the charges? And send me to an Indian prison? I might be better off here.'

McGregor spoke, 'You are a pawn at the end of the day. We need to figure out who coordinated those terror attacks in India. It did result in American deaths too. We need to figure out who killed Khan. And if you help us with that, you will be given protection from them. You will serve your sentence in a minimum security prison, and will then be given witness protection.'

Pascal considered for a moment. 'I shall need it in writing.' McGregor removed his phone. But Mayank stopped him.

Mayank said, 'I am sure you would. But you aren't in a position to make demands. The Arabs will get the information they want from you either way. You give it to us and spare yourself the torture. So you aren't getting squat in writing.'

Pascal blinked first. 'What do you want to know?'

Mayank said, 'Everything. Starting with the story of Prime Minister Khan.'

'Can you at least get me something to wear? It is pretty cold.'

'You are not reciting the *Mahabharat* to me. Once you are done, we will take you out of here.'

'Ok. Ok. About 2 weeks ago, I saw an advert on the Dark Web. It was for a political hit. You could send in your details, quote a price, and then you would have to fly down somewhere. Besides work experience in this...umm...field, there were certain language, look, and passport requirements. I fit the bill on all three.'

McGregor said, 'So, is it like Monster.com for murderers?'

Pascal nodded. 'Pretty much. Not just murders. It's for every kind of crime—it is all about supply and demand. Someone in Hong Kong has a demand for cocaine. Someone in Colombia has the supply. Someone from Spain can facilitate the transfer.'

Mayank asked, 'What's this website?'

'The IP keeps changing. There is no set website. There are some proxies which redirect you. We get the IP through e-mail in the spam folder actually.'

Mayank, 'Ok. Let's get back on track. So you sent in a...err... job application?'

Despite the circumstance, Pascal smiled. 'Yes, I guess so. Then I got an e-mail. It included an e-boarding pass in a new name to Reunion Island for the next day.'

'He was testing you. It would be impossible to get a passport in a fake name in less than 24 hours.'

'No, he was just verifying that I was indeed in France. Even though Reunion Island is in the Indian Ocean, it is a French territory. So to fly from Paris to Reunion is a domestic flight, not an international flight. All I needed was a French driver's license in the new name, not a passport. That can be arranged in a few hours. So I flew down to Reunion.'

Two weeks ago
Reunion Island, Indian Ocean

Although located close to the tourist havens of Maldives and Seychelles, Reunion was hardly on the radar of island-loving tourists. This was a shame, because it offered views which were as spectacular as those of its better known cousins.

As Pascal's Air France plane descended towards the Roland Garros Airport at Saint-Denis, he admired the pristine blue colour of the ocean. *Even if I don't get the gig, at least this will be a decent vacation.*

As expected, customs and immigration was a breeze. What Pascal didn't expect was a man waiting outside for him. He was asked for his name and after checking some ID, he was promptly whisked away in a nondescript grey hatchback.

Pascal passed a number of small picturesque towns. He did not bother enquiring about the final destination. He was on a tiny island; how far could it possibly be, anyway? After a while, he saw signs for a town called 'Le Port'. The man who had driven him, stopped the car outside a community centre.

It was a small town and in the middle of the afternoon of a weekday, the centre would be relatively empty. The man who had driven him reached in the glovebox and gave him a small package. It had a handwritten message on a sticky note. It said:

'On entering the centre, show your French ID and ask for a locker. Put all your belongings in there and wear these swimming trunks. Enter the pool and wait.'

Pascal had no choice but to comply. It was pretty smart. He would be meeting in a secluded albeit public place. There was no chance of him recording this conversation, as he would not have any electronic device in the pool. He followed the instructions. There was no one in the pool.

Soon, a rather small-framed man wearing trunks and swimming goggles jumped in from the opposite side of the pool and swam towards him. '*Bonjour, Jean Pierre.*'

Pascal replied, '*Bonjour, Monsieur.* And you are...'

The man cut him short. 'We will get to that later. Now, should we get to the assignment first?'

'If that's what you prefer.' *No time for BS. That works for me.*

The man said, 'The former Prime Minister of Pakistan is currently seeking refuge in India. We know the exact location he is being held at. Well, he is the target. The security is not very tight.'

Pascal frowned. 'But there must be more to it.'

'Why do you say that?'

Pascal replied, 'You just said that the security is lax. You know the location. You could just contract this out to someone local. Why would you need a specialist like me?'

'Specialist? Now, that's a business-like word. I like it. You are correct. In addition to killing him, it would be required to take his body to the MindCorp office in Mumbai, transfer his memories to the mind of a Chronicler, and bring that Chronicler to me.'

'Why not just back it up in a hard drive?'

The man was obviously prepared. 'Two reasons. Firstly, we need someone we can plug into a neural network—it has to be a human mind. As you know, Chroniclers are highly trained for the job. Secondly, a hard drive is uncomplicated. Kidnapping—now that creates confusion in the minds of the authorities. They have jurisdictional issues. They wonder ceaselessly about motives. The authorities will do a deep dive into the Chronicler's history figuring out whether he is really kidnapped or is complicit in the act. It is a PR disaster for the government. All this confusion buys us time and leverage. Capisce?

Pascal nodded and asked, 'One more thing. Do I bring him to Reunion?'

'Of course not. I shall let you know which place, once the wheels are in motion.'

'Fair enough. But I will need access to funds and personnel. I will design the entire operation and contact you via the Dark

Web. Once you greenlight it and transfer the funds to me, I will execute the project in 24 hours. Of course, there will be a separate expense account over and above my fee.'

The man said, 'You seem fairly confident. I agree. Once I accept the plan, I will wire 25 per cent of the amount to your account. You will get the remaining amount when you deliver the Chronicler to me. Once I greenlight the project, I will also tell you the location to bring him to. This will help you with your exfiltration strategy. Do you have any other questions or doubts?'

Pascal asked, 'I still don't know your name.'

The man replied, 'You can call me Fixer.'

MindCorp, Dubai

'Man, fuck you, Pascal!' From the little he had known McGregor, it seemed like an uncharacteristic response to Mayank.

McGregor looked at Pascal and then at Mayank's rather surprised expression. 'He might as well give us the name "Keyser Soze". This Fixer character has been a myth since years.'

Pascal said, 'That's what even I thought. But the money in my account is real. The kidnapping and the...ahem...project with Khan was real. The assistance I received was real. The instructions I received were real enough too.'

McGregor shook his head. 'I still don't buy...'

Mayank cut him short by pouncing on him and shouting 'DUCK!'

McGregor said, 'What the fuck, Bose...' and then saw the limp body of Pascal. He got up on his fours and crawled towards Pascal.

Mayank got up. 'It's safe to get up now.' He pulled a needle out of Pascal's neck. 'It's poison tipped. I did think that bloody bird looked a little dodgy. I reckon the needle was released from a bird drone which was eavesdropping right by the window. As soon as I saw his head jerk forward, I dived for you. You ok?'

McGregor was shaken. 'Yes, just never been on the field. So were we targets as well?'

Mayank walked around the room and found two more needles. 'If it looks like a duck, walks like a duck, and quacks like a duck, it is most probably a duck. So much for a myth. I can safely tell you McGregor that Fixer is very, very real.'

McGregor was trying to regain his composure. 'Jesus! That's going to raise a few eyebrows in Langley.'

'That's not our immediate problem. Our immediate problem is Udai. We need to find him.'

'Why?'

'Because Fixer will now want Udai and the data. And however resourceful Udai is, this Fixer guy might just be too much to handle for a civilian.'

Manama, Bahrain

Fixer wasn't in the brightest of moods. He seldom missed his chosen target. *Was that Indian, Mayank Bose, that fast? Or was Fixer a fraction slower than usual? Was age catching up with him?* He no longer did it for the money anyway, although the money just kept getting better. He thought of himself as the Roger Federer of his domain; there was nothing to prove to anyone anymore. He just continued to do it on his own terms, because he enjoyed it and he was still one of the best at what he did.

He put his thoughts aside as he logged into a VR video game. Rife with 15-year-olds, the instant messaging apps built into these games were a godsend for his business.

His client logged on to the same channel and they began an instant chat.

Fixer – Welcome.

Client – I understand that we might have a problem.

Fixer – Yes, some unexpected developments. But I am on it.

Client – If you are charging me 200 mill, you better be more than just 'on it'.

Fixer did not like his tone, but the customer was always right.

Fixer – Of course.

Client – Despite the hiccups, will we meet the deadline?

Fixer – I always have a built-in buffer. I will get it done.

Client – There is no room for failure. And that had been made clear to you right at the beginning. I do not wish to remind you of the consequences of failure.

No client had ever rattled Fixer, but then again, he had never quite had a client like this before. He wanted to tell the client to fuck off, but he bit his tongue.

Fixer – I said, I will get it done.

Abruptly, the client left the chat. Fixer knew he would have to pull the trigger quicker than he had planned. He had to get in touch with Udai.

Dubai, UAE

Udai would have preferred to rent a car. But with no documentation, that was impossible. He was considering cabbing it to the neighbouring city of Abu Dhabi, but most cabs these days had cameras and he needed a modicum of anonymity.

So he took a metro to Ibn Batuta station in Dubai, consciously avoiding looking at any cameras. From there he paid 60 dirhams to get a one-way bus ticket to Abu Dhabi. If he had thought that he would blend in easily, he was highly mistaken. The bus was filled with labourers from Asia and Africa, who couldn't afford to travel by cab. Even in his rather

Spartan appearance, he stuck out like a sore thumb. He decided not to make a big deal about it.

He sat next to a Filipino kid and pulled his cap over his eyes. He felt his cell phone buzzing. He was still on the VPN. He flipped out his cell phone and saw that the battery was draining. He would have to buy a charger and a couple of power banks soon.

He had received a new e-mail. He opened it. Simultaneously, the bus started moving and exiting the terminus.

Udai,

Let me apologize for the inconvenience Watson caused you. His real name was Pascal. He won't be a bother anymore, because I have killed him now.

I take it that you like to live. You have proved yourself to be quite resourceful, but your beginner's luck might just run out. However, if you join me, not only will you get to live, I will also handsomely compensate you for your losses. What say?

Fixer

Udai was exhausted and in no mood for all this anymore. He didn't think twice before replying.

Fixer,

*_I_*

Udai

Despite himself, Fixer smiled at the middle finger symbol in the reply. He had expected this. A part of him would have even been a touch disappointed if Udai had buckled right away. *Time to crank up the pressure.*

Washington DC, USA

Deputy Director Emerson was awaiting the arrival of the Secretary of State, Upton, at a quiet bistro close to Blair House. He wondered why he hadn't been called to the office. He would never get used to the cloak-and-dagger style of DC.

Secretary Upton entered a few minutes later than scheduled. He mumbled an apology for being late and exchanged a brief, unfriendly handshake. He got to the point straight away. 'A few hours ago, my office received an e-mail. Suffice to say that it has created more than a flutter in the West Wing.'

Emerson, 'I can assure you, I did not send it.'

Upton leaned in closer. 'I know that. The e-mail stated that this man who killed Prime Minister Khan carries specific secrets about the United States. And not just the Wikileaks kind of secrets which tend to blow over.'

Emerson asked, 'Then, what kind?'

Upton whispered, 'Illegal renditions of detainees to Guantanamo Bay. Drone strikes on civilian areas. And the worst of all—undermining China in Asia.'

'Undermining China?'

Upton leaned back and sighed. 'Yes, and what's at stake is Pax Americana.'

'Pax Americana' referred to American economic and military dominance over the world. It came into being at the end of the World War II.

After the Marshall Plan helped rebuild Europe from the ravages of the two world wars, the old world domination of Britain was over, and Pax Britannica, the global dominance of Great Britain, ended. The current thinking in academic circles which worried many Americans was that Pax Americana would be replaced by 'Pax Sinica'—Chinese global domination.

Emerson was one of the sceptics. America was too big, too powerful for such a foreseeable future. 'Aren't you being paranoid? Britain lost its pre-eminence, because it was financially drained by the two world wars. We aren't in a war with China.'

Upton raised his voice. 'Oh, but we are. Just an economic one. They have developed a new silk route, which is called One Belt One Road. They have invested heavily in Africa, happily propping up regimes we cannot, because of our Human Rights Laws and Ethics Commissions. They have literally taken over Pakistan. This could render our trade routes and shipping lanes obsolete. Whoever controls world trade, controls the world. So, no, I don't think I am being paranoid.'

Emerson posed, 'So what does this have to do with my agency? I thought that in the last meeting we had decided that we will let the Asians handle it, and we only give the Indians a helping hand.'

Upton retorted, 'You have that McGregor fellow there, isn't it? How good is he?'

Emerson said, 'He is a good agent, but on the desk. He has some field training, but he is clearly not cut out for that.'

Upton said, 'Give him all the field support he needs. We are no longer just a helping hand. I want this Udai guy; he has data which is a potential wrecking ball. It would not only set us on a diplomatic collision course with China, but also derail our old relationships with NATO allies in Europe.'

'As you say.'

'But, Emerson, we still keep a low profile. If possible, we need plausible deniability, in case something goes awry. So let the Indians lead this one; after all, the terror attacks happened on their soil. It will give a boost to their egos as well.'

'Got it, sir.'

Dubai, UAE

Chang entered the room and was surprised to see Mayank with a white man. The white man, McGregor, was even more surprised to see a Chinese man enter the room. Confused, he asked, 'You are working with the Chinese on this?'

Mayank said, 'Relax McGregor, he is as Indian as Lucy Liu is an American.'

McGregor still didn't seem convinced. Mayank decided that he didn't need to assuage his curiosity at the moment. There were more pressing matters at hand. Mayank looked at Chang, 'He is McGregor, CIA, and McGregor, this is Chang—he is Indian. We are working together for now. So, Chang, what did you find out at the bank?'

'It's not a very big bank. There were people actually queueing up outside to meet the teller. Most of the clientele is not tech-savvy enough to use the ATMs for deposits or withdrawals. Typical, low-wage labourers are exploited by the Arabs here. When I visited the bank, I saw some of the tellers still using stamp pads; because their clients were not literate enough to sign, they were asking for thumb impressions.'

McGregor said, 'So, a very low-tech operation?'

'Which is very good to move cash around,' said Mayank. 'Earlier, paper trails used to be a problem. Now the bigger problem for crooks is a digital footprint.'

McGregor said, 'But once the money is deposited here, if they have to transfer it to Pakistan, they would still need to electronically wire it. So we can run a trace.'

Chang shook his head. 'Not really. The bank is happy to run a hawala operation.'

Mayank said, 'Don't fucking tell me that you dipped into our funds again. New Delhi is going to be livid.'

Chang shrugged. 'What else could I do?'

'Hang on there. What's a hawala operation?' McGregor asked.

Mayank looked at Chang, who seemed reluctant. 'Ok, Ok. I will be the one to explain.' He turned to McGregor. 'In South Asia, there is an older system for transferring money. It does not require an actual paper trail—that's a Western banking concept. The hawala system works on trust.'

McGregor responded with a 'Huh?'

Mayank continued, 'If I was in Dubai and Chang was in Delhi, and I wanted to send Chang $1000, instead of going through a formal banking route, I would approach a hawala operator and hand him $1000 in cash. That hawala operator would contact another hawala operator in Delhi, who would hand over the $1000, minus the commission, to Chang, again in cash. So this would never enter the banking system, would never be shown as an income, and would thus never be taxed. It's called a parallel or black economy. Heck, the size of India's parallel economy is estimated to be as big as its real economy. Guesses and estimates tend to vary; some urban legends say it is over $100 trillion. And this system is prevalent all over Asia.'

McGregor said, 'So in a nutshell, this money is untraceable.'

Chang shook his head. 'Post 9/11, it is believed that your NSA collected a lot of data on hawala operators in the Middle East and Pakistan.'

'Why?'

'Because that's how Al-Qaeda transferred funds to the US, which ultimately enabled them to execute 9/11.'

McGregor asked, 'There are hawala operators even in the US?'

Mayank cut in. 'Yeah, they are everywhere. That's not the point. The point Chang is making is that we know that Fixer transferred the money. We know which hawala operator it was transferred to in Pakistan. We know the towns where the terrorists train in Pakistan—mostly around Muridke. So, can you get the NSA to give us a list of hawala operators in two or three towns in Pakistan? That would narrow it down. We can look for large sums, a fortnight before and after the terror attacks in India, by putting pressure on Al-Fatah Bank here. We back trace those and we know which group carried out the terror attacks in India.'

McGregor said, 'I am not sure. Are we after Udai, or are we after the guys who conducted the terror attacks?'

Mayank replied, 'It is all fucking linked. The arrival of that damn yacht carrying Khan. His application for refuge. Terror strikes. What if everything is because of what he holds in his mind?'

Abu Dhabi, UAE

Udai looked at the *MindCorp* sign at the Abu Dhabi office from a little supermarket parking lot across the street. He had gotten so far, but how could he possibly go inside and access the neural network? They had almost tripled the security.

He felt a whirring noise above. He looked up to see a drone. He decided to enter the supermarket. He felt his cell phone buzz. He unlocked it—there was a notification for a new e-mail.

Udai,

Good job with the cell phone. Whatever masking software you used, I was unable to trace it. However, you do realize that your choices are both limited and predictable. You need access to the neural network, if you want to get any leverage over anyone.

Multiple intelligence agencies would rather see you dead than fall into enemy hands. And they might just shoot you at sight. You are a ticking time bomb with the data you have.

You must be wondering how I traced you. Where else would you go but the closest neural network? The intelligence agencies are cutting through the red tape. If I alone can trace you so easily, can you imagine how easy it will be for them to do so?

So I reiterate—come to me, and you will live. Else, be prepared for whatever is offered to you by whichever intelligence agency gets hold of you. Why don't you google some images and videos of Guantanamo Bay? That might help you decide.

Fixer

Udai felt pretty stupid. Even though he had used a masking software, he had gone to the city that he was the most likely to go to. His moves could not be more predictable. This Fixer guy was toying with him. The only reason Fixer was keeping him alive was that he needed not only the hard drive with the data, but also needed Udai's brain to be plugged into the neural network.

After working on his cell phone for the next 20 odd minutes, Udai shot a reply.

Fine. I will come to you, but I obviously don't trust you. So I will zip and upload the contents of the hard disk to a cloud account. If I don't check in every 24 hours, my contact will release that data on the Internet. Someone will be able to decode it once it is in the public domain. Are we clear on this?

The reply was almost immediate. That was followed by the exchange of a series of e-mails.

Fixer – Sounds fair. Stay where you are. You will be picked up in an hour.

Udai – No. I am not going to drive through the Arabian desert with one of your men. Plus I need some time to upload the hard disk to a cloud account. What you will do is this—you will send me a self-drive car at my location. And you will tell me the location to drive to. You are free to track me on GPS. You will also place 100,000 US dollars on a series of prepaid travel debit cards.

Fixer – Seems like you are getting smarter. Just so you know, you don't have much space to negotiate here. But ok, stay put. A self-drive car will be sent to you. It might take until tomorrow, so check yourself into a hotel. Don't bother telling me which one, as I shall know it anyway.

Udai – I prefer German sedans.

Fixer – And I prefer blondes. WTF. Do you think I am running an Avis or Hertz? You will get whatever I can get hold of.

Dubai, UAE

In the windowless, fan-less cell of a moving truck, Iqbal Zubair unknotted his tie. He had hardly been there for 10 minutes, but he was distinctly uncomfortable and his sweat glands were in overdrive mode.

Observing him from a one-way glass, McGregor said, 'We should let him sweat a bit more, yeah? About five more minutes before you do your thing.'

Mayank waited for those five minutes, before aggressively opening the door to the cell. McGregor followed him inside. Mayank then kicked the chair as Zubair fell to the floor, with his eyes wide open in horror.

Mayank pointed his finger at the ground. 'You better sit there, Iqbal.'

Zubair managed to mumble, 'Who are you? What have I done?'

'My name is Mayank Bose. I am from a certain agency in India...let's not get into semantics. And I am taking you back to India, after putting you in a shipping container. We are in a truck which is on the way to the harbour. In India, you will be tried for terrorism.' Mayank scratched his head. 'We have a slow judicial process. You will be convicted. You will exhaust the appeal process to the higher courts and the President in about three years. Yeah, that sounds about right. I reckon that in three to three-and-a-half years you will be hanged.' Mayank's tone was so matter of fact, that he could see Zubair's eyes well up.

Zubair looked confused amidst the imminent onslaught of tears. 'What? No? There must be some mistake. I am a simple bank manager. I am not a jihadi. See, I don't even have a beard.'

'You have a stubble!'

'That's still not a beard!'

Mayank said, 'I know all about you, Iqbal Zubair. Your family history from the bylanes of Rawalpindi to how you got into one of the best business schools in Pakistan, majoring in Finance. I even have pictures of your three little boys. I wonder how they would react when they find out that their father is a terrorist!'

Zubair no longer held back his tears. 'I am not a terrorist. Please! Do something.'

Mayank shook his head. 'You facilitated the hawala transfer of a rather large sum of money recently. That money was used to finance the terror attacks on Indian soil. You are their fucking financier, Iqbal. What can I do except bring you to justice?'

Zubair's face lost some colour. 'No, no! I swear I did not know what it was for. I just thought it would be good for business. I was directed to do so from Karachi—I was just doing my job.'

Mayank said, 'Yeah, that's what every captured Nazi soldier said. It's not much of a defence. But I can't stop you from using it in court in India.' He paused for effect. 'Damn, can you imagine being a Pakistani prisoner in an Indian prison? Well, you don't need to imagine, as you will be there soon.' Mayank moved towards the door of the cell.

Zubair pleaded, 'Wait. Wait. There must be something you can do. Please don't do this to me.'

Mayank asked, 'Ok. I want the guy who gave you the money.'

'He didn't give his name.'

'That doesn't seem to bode well for you.'

'But I did capture him on camera.'

McGregor's eyes lit up for a second. No one had caught Fixer on camera. Could this nervous wreck of a buffoon have? He had his doubts, but overconfident men tend to underestimate people like Iqbal Zubair. 'Ok. I am listening.'

Zubair cleared his throat. 'Usually, we don't have problems with hawala; we just take the amounts at the bank. But this man was adamant. He specified that only I should meet him, and that too at a place of his choosing. I found that a bit fishy.'

Mayank raised his eyebrow, 'Really? You found that a fishy request in the middle of conducting your own fishy and illegal hawala operation?'

Zubair put his hands up. 'I know how it looks. But the tone and tenor of this guy just seemed odd. Even the place he called me to meet him.'

'Where?'

'He gave me GPS coordinates. It was in the middle of the desert. He handed me the money he wanted transferred, in a duffel bag.'

'Then how did you capture his picture?'

'Umm...my car has a dash cam. Because it was so bloody hot, I had kept the engine and AC running, which automatically kept the dash cam on. Given his fishy nature, I backed up that trip's video on my cloud account.'

Mayank gave him his cell phone. 'Access it. Show me.'

A minute later, Mayank was looking at what might have been the first captured video of the Fixer. He showed it to McGregor, who whistled. 'Iqbal, you might just be seeing your children again after all.'

One hour later

McGregor beamed, 'We have the bastard!'

Chang looked up, 'That quickly?'

McGregor seemed indignant, 'We are the goddamn United States of America, buddy. We ran a facial recognition software that can even look through disguises and facial hair. Years and years of airport footage is digitally stored.'

Mayank smiled, 'Stop gloating, McGregor. Where is he?'

McGregor removed a rugged-looking tablet from his bag and switched it on. 'That's a rather nondescript house in Manama, Bahrain. We have eyes on him through various drones.'

Chang asked, 'And can we hear him?'

McGregor punched something into the tablet. 'We have something called Worm Bugs. What you are seeing on your screen is our worms making their way through the plumbing of this guy's house.'

As Chang and Mayank watched in awe, they counted eight worm bugs emerge from various plumbing outlets. The worms then got together in a synchronized fashion and a light on the tablet turned green.

McGregor continued, 'So, these together formed one bug. We have a total of 80 worms, which would give us 10 bugs, spread in strategic locations across his house. The whole process should be done in an hour at the most.'

Mayank looked at Chang, his eyes still wide in amazement. He then turned to McGregor and said, 'All right, McGregor. I guess you have every right to gloat now.'

Abu Dhabi, UAE

So much for a German sedan. The Arab world was bursting at its seams with fancy cars and Fixer had sent him a crappy French Peugeot. *The bastard must have put in a GPS tracker somewhere.*

As he put his seatbelt on, he heard an unfamiliar cellular ringtone. He opened the glovebox and pulled out what looked like a cheap prepaid Android phone. He answered.

'Fixer?'

There was no greeting. Just a set of instructions from Fixer. 'Yes. Get yourself to Manama, Bahrain, and then wait for my instructions. I've sent you a small car with a full tank of petrol. But in case you need more, there are 10 prepaid MasterCards loaded with $10,000 each. Just as you requested—a full $100,000. Each of them has the same PIN: 9956. You can verify the amount on each at any ATM. I am tracking you on GPS, so no funny moves. Drive safe.'

Dubai, UAE

As the three of them watched the proceedings from Manama, Chang looked at Bose and winked. 'He has Udai too.'

Mayank nodded absentmindedly. Clearly something else was playing on his mind. Chang asked, 'So should we wait for Udai to get to Bahrain and then nab this Fixer?'

Mayank shook his head. 'The thought crossed my mind. But Fixer is a slippery bastard. Udai is smart, but he is a corporate drone. If we have the chance, we should grab Fixer.'

'Do we have anyone in Bahrain?'

'Of course, we don't. We don't have the money or the resources to have presence in every country.' He turned to McGregor, 'But our American friends have no such problems.'

McGregor rolled his eyes, 'What? You want us to apologize for being rich and resourceful?'

'No, humility is not a very American trait.'

'But cynicism seems to be a very Indian one.'

Chang intervened, 'Can we please get back on track? McGregor, can you pick Fixer up?'

McGregor said, 'Yes. And while I will let you interview him first, he will be in American custody and will be an American prisoner. We will fly him to the US to face trial.'

Chang said, 'But...'

Mayank cut him off. 'We can do nothing about that, Chang. They arrest him, he is theirs.'

Chang said, 'What about Udai?'

McGregor looked at both of them. 'He is an Indian citizen. He is not wanted for a crime. I will help you nab him; he is yours. But I want access to him and all the memories, not just those concerning America, but all of them. And these are orders from the very top; this is not negotiable.'

Mayank said, 'Seems fair.'

Manama, Bahrain

Fixer took great pride in working alone. He always sourced criminal help for his projects, but no resource was ever in his permanent employ. He almost never repeated the people he hired. There were enough criminals in the world for that, and there was enough unemployment for that as well.

This had given him an edge, a mobility that had helped him become a global operator who serviced everyone—from crooks to dictators. As he watched the CIA men surround his modest villa in Manama, he allowed himself a wry smile. *Being a lone wolf has always been my asset. I guess it is almost poetic that it has today become my Achilles' heel.*

He looked at all his computer equipment and wondered if he should delete all the data before the CIA got in. *Fuck it,* he thought. He then nonchalantly pulled out a Glock 26 from his drawer and put the safety off. *Fixer has never been caught and that's not about to change today.* He then shot himself in the mouth.

48 hours later
New Delhi, India

Chang had always wondered what it would feel like to face a firing squad. As McGregor, Mayank, and Chang sat facing Defence Minister Raman and State Secretary Upton, at the American Embassy in New Delhi, Chang thought that today he had a bit of an inkling.

Upton spoke first. 'So you had Fixer. But he somehow just decided to shoot himself in the mouth as soon as he realized that the game was up.'

McGregor replied, 'Well, he knew he would spend the rest of his natural life behind bars. It is pretty narcissistic of him, if you think about it.'

Upton got up and sat on the table. 'Oh, I've thought about it a lot, McGregor. And in no thoughts of mine, you come out smelling like roses. Do we know his identity?'

McGregor replied, 'Well, we found multiple passports and national identity cards. But we haven't been able to pinpoint any one of them as his one true identity.'

Upton asked, 'Jesus Christ! McGregor, what about his computer files?'

McGregor said, 'Well, that's a bit of a silver lining. He didn't delete anything. I guess once he decided he was gonna blow his brains out, he didn't really care much about it.'

Upton's face showed some relief. 'That's good. That's good. So what do we know?'

McGregor answered, 'He didn't delete anything. But his hard drive and data are still encrypted. All the hardware is being worked on in Langley. We made a copy and gave it to the Indians too—in case they can crack it before us.'

Secretary Upton rolled his eyes, 'Thanks, you are quite the diplomat.'

Defence Minister Raman, who was listening patiently, turned her attention towards the Indians. 'What about Udai?'

Chang looked sheepishly at Mayank. Mayank put his hand on his forehead, rubbed his temples and said, 'Well, he gave us the slip.'

Raman replied, 'Yes, Mayank I read your curt report. It said: "Udai Singh Sodha gave us the slip." I can read English, you know. I am asking you, how did that happen?'

Chang said, 'Well, madam, we were waiting for him at Manama. We even tracked his car on Fixer's phone via a GPS tracker. But when the CIA surrounded his car and brought him in, it was a different man.'

'What? How did that happen?'

Mayank said, 'Well, it is almost an 8-hour drive from Abu Dhabi to Manama. The route cuts across Saudi Arabia.

It seems that Udai halted at this small town called Salwa, which is near the Saudi-Qatar border. At the gas station there, he paid a Sri Lankan guy $500 to drive his rented Peugeot to Manama.'

Raman raised her eyebrows, 'So the CIA arrested a random Sri Lankan guy?'

'Yes, madam.'

'So now, you have no idea where Udai is?'

'Nope. But he can't possibly know that Fixer is dead.'

Just then an eager intern stepped into the meeting room. Secretary Upton snapped at him. 'I specifically said not to be disturbed during this meeting. And who the hell are you, kid?'

'I am Paul, the intern.'

'Well, Paul, the intern, this is a closed-door meeting. You must be in the wrong room.'

'No, no, sir. I was specifically asked to come here and ask all of you to switch on the news.' He pointed to the LED in the room.

Upton said, 'Christ—what's happened now. Ok, Paul, please switch it on.'

Paul was clearly nervous and McGregor putting a friendly arm on his shoulder didn't calm his nerves. After fumbling across a few channels, he found CNN International.

The ticker at the bottom said: 'BREAKING NEWS! PAKISTAN SUSPENDS ALL AMERICAN AND INDIAN DIPLOMATIC VISAS.'

On the screen, Ambassador Jie Huang was addressing the press in his sing-song English. 'It is our belief that Americans and Indians are involved in sabotaging the One Belt One Road initiative of the People's Republic of China. In light of this, after consultation with the officials of the Islamic Republic of Pakistan, Pakistan is temporarily suspending all diplomatic ties with the United States and India. Their citizens have 48 hours to vacate the country and all diplomatic visas are being cancelled.'

Mayank asked, 'Well, shouldn't this announcement be made by a representative of the Government of Pakistan?'

Defence Minister Raman replied, 'They are no longer even bothering with the façade. They want us to know, they are in control. And now they have dispensed with diplomatic protocol. This is unusual, but the Chinese want to make a point.'

Upton turned to McGregor, 'What the fuck is this, McGregor? What are the ramifications?'

McGregor scratched his stubble. 'Where do I begin? For starters, it affects our supply routes to NATO forces in landlocked Afghanistan.'

Ms Raman spoke, 'Don't worry about that. We can get you an alternate route through our Chahbahar port in Iran.'

Upton said, 'Thank you, Minister, but as you know, our relationship with Iran is still frosty. But then again, we may have no choice. The President doesn't want to give Iran much leeway. This is bad.' He turned back to McGregor, 'What else?'

'Well, we have bases there since SEATO and CENTO** days. We are involved with various agencies overtly and covertly. We have assets on the ground there, who are Pakistani citizens. We have multiple humanitarian initiatives dealing with water and

** The Southeast Asia Treaty Organization (SEATO) was an international organization for collective defence in Southeast Asia created by the Southeast Asia Collective Defense Treaty, or Manila Pact, signed in September 1954 in Manila, Philippines. Primarily created to block further communist gains in Southeast Asia, SEATO is generally considered a failure, because internal conflict and dispute hindered general use of the SEATO military.
The Central Treaty Organization (CENTO), originally known as the Baghdad Pact or the Middle East Treaty Organization (METO), was a military alliance of the Cold War. It was formed in 1955 by Iran, Iraq, Pakistan, Turkey, and the United Kingdom, and dissolved in 1979.

sanitation. And there are probably other things that I've not thought of.'

Mayank spoke, 'But the timing of all of this, just when we raid Fixer's place, strikes me as odd. Isn't it?'

McGregor shook his head, 'For one dead guy? You think China would pick a fight with its two rivals over one dead guy?'

Mayank said, 'But they don't know he is dead. Only we do. For them, it is complete radio silence. For all they know, he might be singing like a canary to us. They have the satellite imaging to know we barged into that home in Bahrain. But that's it. They wouldn't know he killed himself.'

McGregor said, 'So they pulled the trigger first. Now, if we really had Fixer and he was giving us all the information...'

Secretary Upton continued for him, '...the Chinese would say that we are just making things up after they threw out our diplomats and citizens. It gives them plausible deniability. Even if we raise a hue and cry at the UN, China always has a veto and enough votes from its lackeys in Asia and Africa.'

Chang asked, 'So, what now?'

Raman said, 'The key to this entire puzzle is in the mind of Udai. I don't care how, but you better find him.'

Embassy of the People's Republic of China, Islamabad, Pakistan

At this time, General Ahmed had no patience for diplomatic niceties. He did not knock on the door or wait to be ushered in.

He simply took a seat opposite the Chinese Ambassador and said, 'Are you bloody insane, Ambassador?' He did not even acknowledge the presence of Colonel Lin.

Ambassador Huang was duly prepared. 'What do you mean?'

'The local press have been calling you "the Viceroy". You are not really the Viceroy. I sincerely hope that you know that.' He thumped the desk before continuing, 'How did you think you could take unilateral diplomatic decisions without consulting the Pakistan Army? What if the Americans just bomb us? Or the Indians cross the LoC?'

Colonel Lin said, 'Relax, General. Neither of these scenarios seem to occur in our simulations.'

'I don't trust my grandchild with a Chinese toy. You think I trust your military simulations?'

The faces of both the Chinese men turned a hue of red. Ambassador Huang spoke, 'You do know that you are replaceable.'

The General was not about to back down. 'You do know, you are in my country? More than half a million Pak troops report to me. You have a presence of a few thousand people. In your entire history, you have never conquered another nation. You really want to take us on?'

Colonel Lin smiled, 'You fool. You are already conquered. Let's say, you round the few thousand Chinese people here and send them back to Beijing. Then what do you reckon will happen?'

The General did not answer.

Ambassador Huang replied, 'Forget your debts, your country doesn't have money to pay interest on the loans you have taken from us, the Saudis, the Americans, and the IMF. We will just call in the loans. You will default. The rest of your creditors will call in the loans. Again, you will default. Your currency will collapse. There will be hyperinflation like in Venezuela or Zimbabwe. Except Venezuela had oil and Zimbabwe really had no enemies. Who is ever going to bail you out?'

General Ahmed glared at both the Chinese men.

Colonel Lin intervened, 'So, General, I beg to differ. China has conquered you. And you better toe our line. You publicly support us, and within 12 months, we will even declare you Field Marshal.'

General Ahmed did not say anything. He got up and left.

Ambassador Huang turned to Colonel Lin, 'All of this is a huge gamble.'

Lin replied, 'Empires are built by taking gambles, not by playing safe.'

Mumbai, India

Aditi was driving to the grocery store when a traffic constable stopped her.

He handed her a breathalyzer. 'Madam, random check for drunk driving.'

Aditi looked at him incredulously. She pointed at her watch. 'At 2 in the afternoon?'

She didn't think much of it and blew into the apparatus. He looked at her and said, 'Madam, it is positive. Please get out of the car.'

'That's ridiculous.'

He gestured to two lady constables who forced Aditi out and took her to the Magistrate's van that issued summons for those caught drunk driving.

'Get in, Madam.'

Aditi reluctantly got in, only to see Mayank Bose and Chang waiting for her inside the van.

Mayank said, 'I really am sorry about this.'

She just went ahead and slapped him across the face. He winced in pain. 'Ok, I deserve that. But we couldn't take the chance of inviting you to our office and you refusing. You cooperate with us and all charges will be dropped. Else, the Magistrate is going to send you in for 6 months for drunk driving.'

She slapped him again. 'Ok, I deserve that too.'

Chang covered his cheeks as he asked, 'Can you just hear us out? We are on your side.'

Riyadh, Saudi Arabia

Udai was used to the heat and humidity of Mumbai, but Saudi Arabia was something else. The journey in the back of a transport van had been uneventful, but arduous. He had paid a driver $50 in cash to ferry him to Riyadh in a transport van filled with employees of some American oil company. *Poor souls—they looked more like slave labour than employees, even as the coffers of American and British oil companies continued to overflow.*

Udai had switched off his cell phone completely for the duration of the journey, in the fear of being traced. Surely by now Fixer would have realized that he had given him the slip. He got off near the outskirts of the capital, Riyadh, and made his way to a small department store where he changed his attire and bought a new cap.

He found a WiFi zone and connected his cell phone. A few years ago, the rules of gender segregation had been relaxed in Saudi Arabia, but the men and women still sat separately. *Old habits die hard.* He sat in a men's section where some Arab kids were playing the latest shooting game. Every generation had at least one iconic shooting video game. *It is in human nature to want to satiate some bloodthirst, just like survival is inherent to human nature. No better example than himself.*

As soon as he connected to the WiFi, a series of voice messages came in from Aditi. There were a total of 14 voice messages left in his e-mail inbox. The first one showed concern, the last one indicated a full blown panic attack. *She is a strong girl; there must have been a catalyst.*

He made a VoIP call to her.

She answered at the first ring. 'Udai, are you all right?'

'I am ok. A bit tired, but I'm alive. Don't worry.'

'But where are you?'

'I'd rather not say—it's safer that way for both of us.'

She hesitated. 'There is someone here who wants to talk to you.' She handed the phone to Mayank.

'Udai, this is Mayank Bose. I am speaking on behalf of the Indian government.'

'I really don't give a fuck.'

Mayank looked at Aditi as he spoke into the phone. 'You two truly are made for each other.'

'What do you want?'

'I think you know.'

'You aren't getting anything. For all I know, you are a Pakistani spy, who has kidnapped my wife.'

'Well, why don't you ask her?'

'Wow, you truly are an idiot. Why would she say otherwise, while in your captivity?'

Mayank sounded exasperated, 'Listen to me. There are people who want that data. And those people would have no qualms killing you to get it. We want to exfiltrate you from wherever you are and bring you home safely. You can only access the data from a MindCorp site. It's just a series of binaries to you at the moment. I know you have been through a lot. We want to help.'

'If you wanted to help, you would have sounded the alarm when I was taken from MindCorp in Mumbai. There was no mention of me. So stop feigning interest in my well-being. I know you want the data. I just don't fucking trust you.'

'How can we change that? I want you to trust me. Trust your country.'

'Fine. Tell me, who wants the data? And who is willing to kill me to get it?'

Mayank realized it was a tough call. But he had to let this information out to a civilian. In all fairness, this civilian was in the vortex of this mess. 'Ok. We have a reasonably strong hunch based on circumstantial evidence...'

'For crying out loud, you sound like a EULA agreement I have to accept, when I install a new software. Who is it?'

'The Chinese.'

There was no reply at the other end. Mayank thought that he had lost the line and asked, 'Hello... Udai, are you still there?'

After a few seconds, Udai replied, 'Yes, I am here. I want the Prime Minister or the Defence Minister to announce in a press conference that an Indian citizen named Udai Sodha has been kidnapped from MindCorp, and that you are doing everything in your power to bring him back.'

'Don't be ridiculous. We have never publicly acknowledged your kidnapping. It is too late now.'

'Yeah, I guess it is too late now.' Udai disconnected the phone.

Mayank looked at Aditi. 'Where did you find him?'

Beijing, China

The four seniormost members of the Communist Party's politburo were polite, but firm. Only one of them asked questions, which the others silently watched, deciding to talk only if required.

Premier Xi wasn't very comfortable. He had purged most of his opponents and considered these men loyal, so the questions were unexpected.

'What happens if the US throws out Chinese diplomats? And the NATO countries follow suit?'

Xi replied, 'It will not come to that.'

The old man continued, 'What about trade sanctions?'

'Our economy is strong enough to withstand the pressure exerted by the imperialist West. I assure you.'

'What about India?'

'They have never attacked anyone. Their ridiculous democracy ensures that they are always fighting amongst themselves. They are the least of our concerns.'

Not all the members look convinced. One of them said, 'Remember one thing, Premier Xi, it has taken decades and decades to build China into an economic powerhouse. We have supported your One Belt One Road initiative as it would take us to the greatest of heights. But we wonder, if you fail and undo those decades of hard work, what will be the choice before this politburo?' He let the threat hang in the air.

Xi bowed slightly. 'I can assure the politburo, it will not come to that.'

Xi got up and escorted the elderly men out of the office. He rushed back to his desk and called up Colonel Lin. 'Have you found that Indian?'

'Not yet.'

'I won't let the future of my presidency be decided by the actions of some random Indian idiot with low IQ! You find him!'

Lin had read Udai's file. His IQ was through the roof. But sometimes silence is golden. 'Yes, we will get on it right away.'

Riyadh, Saudi Arabia

Udai realized that he was about to take a big gamble. If he was online for a long time, he risked being tracked. But he had run out of options.

He went to an IT store and picked up an off-the-shelf Acer laptop and a plug-in DNA reader. He went online at a WiFi zone and then installed a VPN service to mask his location and set his IP address to Fiji. He then proceeded to make sure he was not connected in any way to a cloud account in his own name. Finally, he downloaded the TOR browser—the regular Chrome or Firefox wouldn't suffice for his needs.

He tried opening the Silk Route site. *Bullseye.* He was on the Dark Web. There were many websites he could now access which were not available or were practically unknown to almost all Internet users. It was believed that over 90 per cent of our usual websites can only be accessed through the Dark Web. You could source anything—from drugs to prostitutes to stolen antiques. Instead of .com, the sites always ended with .onion on the Dark Web.

The search engine DuckDuckGo was the Google of the Dark Web. It led him to a Russian website called RAMP—an abbreviation for Russian American Marketplace. He found a listing for what he was looking for—Rosetta Stone.

Long believed to be a myth, many people wondered if it even existed. It was rumoured to have been developed by a Norwegian teenager. It drew its name from the ancient Greek tablet which led to the deciphering of the Egyptian hieroglyphs. The software was supposed to be a universal translator, and it deciphered all encrypted data. Udai wanted to access the memories of Khan without plugging himself into a neural network.

He clicked on the hyperlink for Rosetta Stone.

A few minutes later, a messenger popped up on his screen and a chat window opened. Like all marketplaces, there was bargaining involved. The handle's name was @NordicWarrior. Udai wondered if he was really Norwegian or was he just perpetuating the myth of the software's Norwegian origin.

@NordicWarrior – *How long do you need it for?*

Udai – At least a couple of hours

@NordicWarrior – *Wow. Usually people want it for a few minutes.*

Udai – I understand. But I need it for 2 hours, right now. Maybe more, later.

@NordicWarrior – *That will cost you $30,000.*

Udai – And I will pay you 15.

@NordicWarrior – *Let's settle at 20.*

Udai – Done.

@NordicWarrior – *You will put in the full amount in* RAMP's *escrow account. If* Rosetta *is not able to decipher your software, you will get your money back. If it does, you lose the full amount even if you use it for just 5 mins.*

Udai – Has it ever failed? How do I know you won't access my data yourself?

@NordicWarrior – *If you are a lonely man and want to make small talk, I recommend Tinder. Do you agree to my terms?*

Udai – Yes.

Udai used two of the prepaid MasterCards that Fixer had given him to deposit $20,000 into RAMP's escrow account.

He got access to Rosetta Stone. He uploaded the data from the external hard drive. As soon as the data was uploaded, the decrypter tool popped up. Those were the longest 20 minutes of his life.

Finally, a screen popped up.

'DECRYPTION SUCCESSFUL'

A virtual clone of the MindCorp neural network popped up. The screen said, 'Please confirm DNA match.'

Udai plugged in the DNA reader and then pressed his palm on the device. The screen said, 'DNA Match Confirmed.' On the right hand corner, a countdown timer of 120 minutes began. He clicked on 'Play' and started viewing the memories of Prime Minister Khan. *Oh, for some popcorn.*

New Delhi, India

The Defence Minister looked aghast at the suggestion made by Mayank on the other end of the video call.

'We can't possibly reveal now that he was kidnapped. The opposition will go to every channel and say we deliberately misled the people of this country.'

Mayank understood the political ramifications, but he was hoping that Minister Raman would be able to see past that. 'I sincerely don't know much about politics, madam. What I can tell you is that these are his demands. He thinks we threw him under the bus when we didn't reveal his kidnapping to the world. And frankly, I don't blame him.'

She didn't look convinced. 'What are his options? He can't saunter into any MindCorp location; all of them are monitored. You have his wife. He has been smart. Even if he has the will, does he have the resources?'

Mayank replied, 'In a way, I agree with you. But we can't wait for him to run out of resources, patience, or will. Something triggered the Chinese and I am willing to bet that whatever triggered them is in the memories currently in Udai's possession. What if they get to him first? What could be so important that the Chinese would risk taking on the Americans and us, simultaneously, in a diplomatic war?'

The Minister hesitated. 'Yes, that is a concern. Let me see what I can do.'

A few hours later, a Home Ministry spokesperson invited a select band of journalists to Shastri Bhavan in New Delhi. He held up a piece of paper. 'I will read a statement from the Home Minister. I will not be taking any questions at the moment.' He then began to read—

'An Indian citizen named Udai Singh Sodha, who happens to be an employee of MindCorp, has been reported missing since an incident occurred at their office in Mumbai. The circumstances under which he went missing are being investigated, but the indications are that he may have been kidnapped. Earlier reports of him being involved in the assassination of former Pakistani Prime Minister, Ishtiaq Khan, are unfounded. MindCorp is extending all information and cooperation to the government as is being asked. We intend to resolve this issue very soon and will do all we can to reunite Mr Sodha with his family.'

As the reporters began to raise their hands to ask questions, the spokesperson waved at them and walked off.

Mumbai, India

24 hours later, as they watched the statement on television, Chang asked Mayank, 'That's good. He got what he wanted?'

Mayank fiddled with a paperweight on his desk. 'Not quite. He asked for the Prime Minister or the Defence Minister. This is the Home Ministry. I hope he understands the political compulsions behind that move.'

Aditi entered their office and Chang immediately got up. 'You heard back from him?'

Aditi smiled. 'Won't you bastards like to know? Good that I found you at your office. It means you are not harassing and blackmailing women drivers.'

Mayank said, 'I wonder how long you will continue to play the harassed damsel-in-distress card. It really doesn't suit you.'

Aditi rolled her eyes. 'Anyway, I have to relay a message from Udai before I head to the airport.'

Chang said, 'Who said you can head to the airport? You can't leave the city.'

'Actually, I am leaving the country.'

Mayank looked confused. 'You can't do that. He just told you. Where are you planning on going?'

'Tel Aviv.'

'What?'

'Tel Aviv, Israel.'

'I know where it is. But...' It then dawned on him. 'Udai has reached Israel!'

She nodded. 'I think you better have a chat with Udai.' She handed him her phone. 'No need to use a VoIP service. He has an Israeli number. Check the last dialled one.'

He looked at the last dialled list. 'The one with the country code +972?'

'Yes.'

He dialled the number. Udai immediately answered. 'Hello?'

'Udai, this is Mayank Bose. Your wife Aditi is here.'

'Oh, good.'

'She said you have something to tell me?'

'More like give you a set of instructions.'

Mayank rolled his eyes. 'Sure. What?'

'Drop all of your frivolous drinking charges against Aditi. Then have her escorted to the airport. She will board the 8 pm flight on El Al to Tel Aviv. Once she is out of Indian airspace, you will arrange a video call for me with everyone. And I mean everyone who is a stakeholder in my situation—India, USA, and officials at MindCorp—the whole merry-go-round. I would assume that includes a few ministers and top bureaucrats as well.'

'Are you drunk?'

'You better hope I am not.'

'Ok. Let's say I do all this for you. Seems unlikely, but let's assume I do. What do I get in return?'

'How does all of Kashmir sound to you?'

Mayank was rendered speechless. After gathering his wits, he realized that Udai was enjoying being the hunter instead of the hunted. He allowed himself a smile. 'You cracked it. You accessed the memories of Khan. And you got to Tel Aviv. Fine. I will do as you ask. But I want ALL the details. All of them, once Aditi is airborne and out of Indian airspace.'

Mayank looked at Chang, and then at Aditi. He asked, 'How the hell did he get to Tel Aviv?'

3 years ago
Goa, India

The Russian looked at the bloodied nose of the man seated opposite him. He gestured to the bouncer with a flick of his fingers. The bouncer handed the bleeding man a kerchief. The Russian said, 'Show me your wallet.'

The man was still wiping his blood off, but managed to pass his wallet across the table. The Russian opened it and looked at the IDs and cards. 'Elad Nachman from Haifa, Israel.'

Elad looked at him and nodded. 'Yeah, that's me.'

'Why do you Israelis come to Goa and think you own it?'

Elad said, 'I guess we share that with you Russians.'

The Russian gestured at the bouncer who was glad to land another blow on Elad's face. The Russian said, 'I wonder if that's you talking or your drugs and alcohol. Can never be sure with you lot.'

Elad was clearly in pain. 'What do you want?'

The Russian looked at him incredulously. '*What do I want?* I want my money, motherfucker! In the last four hours, you have lost $29,000 in here, at the blackjack table. And that is not even including the drinks.'

Elad said, 'Yeah, I thought the amount was in rupees. We are in India after all.'

The Russian looked at Elad and hit his desk with his fist. 'What the fuck am I going to do with 29,000 rupees? My driver's salary is more than that. The board outside clearly states—"Only US dollars accepted. Please exchange your pounds and euros or any other currency into US dollars."'

Elad looked at the bouncer and gestured to him to go easy by holding his palm up straight. He then turned his gaze towards the Russian, 'I don't think that sounds very legal in India.'

The Russian laughed, 'What exactly looked legal to you when you entered the premises? We don't even allow Indians in here.'

'So, it is both illegal and racist.'

The Russian asked, 'Yes, we tried communism and equality. That didn't really work. I am not discussing morals with you, fucker. I want my money.'

'I don't have it.'

'Then we make an example of you and you die a slow, painful death.' The Russian once again looked at the bouncer and nodded.

The bouncer removed a hammer from his pocket. Elad's eyes widened. 'What the fuck? He keeps a hammer in his pocket? Who does that?' As he watched the hammer being raised, Elad said, 'Ok, ok. Wait. Let me at least try to get the money.'

The Russian said, 'The hammer always works. That's why it is kept in the pocket.' The bouncer handed Elad his phone.

Elad gladly took the phone. 'Hi, Udai. Sorry to disturb you at this time. I know we've just met, but I don't really have any friends in India yet.'

The Russian interjected, 'I thought you were calling a friend.'

Elad put a finger to his lips asking the Russian to keep quiet. 'I need 29,000 dollars. Like right now. I will pay you back, I promise.'

Elad continued, 'Yes, I do—registered to my number. Wait, you already did? Man, I can't thank you enough. Good night.'

Elad opened his digital wallet registered to his cell phone account. It had just been credited with $29,000. He showed the screen to the Russian.

'This guy, whom you don't even know, transferred 29,000 dollars to your account?'

'Yes, it seems so.'

'I need a friend like that. Next time, bring him.'

'He is Indian.'

'I make exception for good Indians. You bring him.'

Elad shrugged. 'Whatever, man. Where do I transfer the amount?' The Russian gave him a number.

Elad then asked, 'Can I have my stuff back?'

The Russian said, 'Wait! That only covered your gambling. Your bill for the drinks is still pending. That's another 5000 dollars.'

'What? I don't have that...'

The Russian looked at the bouncer. 'Remove the hammer.'

As Elad winced, both the Russian and the bouncer started laughing. The Russian said, 'Relax. I was just messing with you. You should really read the board. For billing over 20,000 dollars, drinks are on the house. Enjoy. Have a few more if you want.'

Previous day

Udai didn't even realize that the two hours for using Rosetta Stone were up. The timer popped up on his screen, while he was in the middle of watching some more of Khan's memories. *This is gold.* He realized that there was such information in these memories that any major country in the world would die to get its hands on, and even kill for. If he kept this data, he would have a permanent target drawn on his back.

India did not have a witness protection plan and they couldn't even protect the Pakistani Prime Minister. The Americans were unpredictable, they might trump up some charge, and send him to Guantanamo Bay or any of their rendition facilities. No one in his right mind could possibly trust the Chinese. Or the Russians, for that matter. Some Western European or South American country might give him refuge, but he would always be in danger of being tracked and whisked off by one of the powers. He thought of Julian Assange and how Ecuador withdrew his asylum status and handed him over to the British authorities. There was only one country in the world that could flip the middle finger to all the global powers and do what it wanted. And no one would dare to take them on. Israel.

He made a VoIP call to Elad; it was time to call in the favour.

'Hi, Elad. This is Udai.'

Elad sounded both surprised and relieved. 'Udai. Damn. I am so glad you are ok. All of us have been concerned, but HQ had told us to seal our lips and not talk to the press.'

'Yes, I think I figured that.'

'Anyway, what can I do?'

'Uh... You know, I've never called in the favour. I never intended to anyway. But I am in a bit of a soup.'

Elad said, 'Hey buddy. It's not of your own making. You were just at the wrong place at the wrong time. What do you need from me?'

'You once told me your dad was in Mossad.'

'Yeah, he is an ex-Mossad. Lives in a nice house on the outskirts of Tel Aviv, now that he is retired.'

'I need political refuge in Israel. I have something to trade.'

'Man, Udai, you sound like James freaking Bond. What can you possibly trade?'

'How about Pakistani troop movements in the Middle East? Those are the guys the Arabs use as cannon fodder for their wars. How about associations in Saudi Arabia and Pakistan which funnel funds to Hamas? How about names and locations of heads of various outfits which chant "Death to Israel" all day long?'

'Jesus!'

'Not only must you mention these to Jesus, you need to get me to his home base.'

Two hours later, with a fake passport, Udai was on a Royal Jordanian flight from Riyadh to Amman. After clearing immigration at Amman, he was escorted to an unremarkable black station wagon outside the airport.

The man seated next to him extended his hand. 'I am Daniel Levison. You better have what you have promised. It seems a lot of strings were pulled to get you here. If you can't deliver what you promised, we will hand you over to the Indian authorities.'

Udai smiled. 'Shalom. Let's get to Tel Aviv first.'

Levison tapped the driver on the shoulder. 'Let's go.'

Four days later
Islamabad, Pakistan

As the chartered Learjet hit the tarmac on the runway in Islamabad, Chang mused to himself, *I could get used to private jets.* In India, he had to struggle to get his bosses to approve a plane ticket. They would rather send him by train. But once the Americans came in, it was like Christmas and Diwali all year long.

The steward handed him his jacket and a range of ties to choose from. As he contemplated, McGregor emerged from the cockpit. 'Chang, just pick one. You are not participating in a beauty contest for crying out loud.'

Chang picked a red tie. 'Communist enough, eh?' he asked McGregor.

McGregor ignored the question. 'We are waiting right here. Four hours is all you have. We don't have an exfil plan, so whatever happens, you get your ass down here. If you think you are going to be arrested, you send me a message from your phone. And we will get the fuck out of here.'

'Thanks. Aren't you just a ray of sunshine? You just boosted my confidence.'

Chang stepped out of the aircraft and was greeted on the tarmac by a bearded Pakistani soldier in uniform. The soldier greeted Chang.

'General Ahmed has asked me to take you to him. I am Major Faiz.'

The Major pointed at a luxury sedan. Chang looked at the car, but could not make out the make, let alone the model. 'What car is this, Major Faiz?'

The soldier said, 'It's a Hongqi H7. I don't even know if I am pronouncing it right. Through a new directive issued by Ambassador Huang, all government vehicles are now Chinese.'

'That's fantastic.'

The soldier didn't look convinced. 'Hardly. The bloody thing is a piece of rubbish. The country hates the Chinese. They are putting up Chinese signs everywhere. Chinese expats and diplomats are quickly buying up the best real estate in our cities and cordoning them off.'

'That bad?'

'Some people are saying it is like the British Raj. Areas cordoned off. Signs in language we don't understand. Different set of rules. No offence, but you are not Chinese. You are Canadian, right?'

'Major, would it matter even if I was Indian?'

The Major shook his head. 'No. Anyone would be better than this lot. Our founding fathers did not fight for a homeland so that we would eventually become a colony again.'

An hour later, Chang was seated in the Islamabad Serena, opposite General Ahmed. Chang noticed that the General's eyes were red. *Is it lack of sleep?* He noticed the whisky glass in front of the General, at 2 in the afternoon. *Or maybe the single malt.*

'General, thanks for seeing me on such short notice.'

'Chang, my boy. You got my brother and nephew Canadian passports at such short notice. My wife and kids have also been relocated to Toronto. And you transferred not an insignificant amount of money into my account. It would be very inhospitable of me to refuse this meeting.' He took a sip. 'You want a drink?'

Chang nodded his head. 'Just a masala chai.'

The General looked up with a hint of surprise. 'Masala Chai?'

'General, I am not Canadian. Or Chinese. I am Indian. Hence, the masala chai.'

The General frowned. 'What? But how? You look...'

'I am an ethnic Chinese from Calcutta. I work for RAW.' The General got up. Chang quickly added, 'Before you do something rash, General, hear me out. I have been frisked and am unarmed. Your family has been escorted to Canada. I bring you a deal from my leadership. It even has the blessings of the US.'

The General reluctantly sat down. Chang said, 'Thanks.'

General Ahmed glared. 'You have 5 minutes before I walk out. And if you didn't have my family in Canada, I would have had you skinned.'

'I know. Now listen carefully, General. The terror attacks in India were ordered by the Chinese, but not by the guys who are here—Ambassador Huang and Colonel Lin. There is an internal power struggle in China to overthrow Xi. A war with India would weaken Xi, as already their resources are stretched.'

'And Prime Minister Khan?'

'That hit was ordered by Xi and the men here.'

'But why?'

'In 1999, Khan was a minister during the Bus diplomacy initiated by Vajpayee, the then Prime Minister of India. He was the last surviving member of that meeting on either side. There was a secret agreement signed between the two sides, but the Kargil war put that on the backburner. Then you had one of your coups and your military took over.'

'What secret agreement?'

'We will get to that. It is quite evident that you are not very happy with the Chinese presence here. They are even replacing road signs in English with Mandarin signs!'

'Yes, they are deeply unpopular.'

'We didn't know about the existence of the agreement till yesterday. That was the bargaining chip Prime Minister Khan had. After a man named Udai accessed the memories of Khan, we started looking for our copy of the agreement. We found it buried in one of the files from that era in the Prime Minister's office. Everything is digital now, but certain files had never been digitized. This was one of them. Thanks to the memory of Khan, we know where your copy of the agreement is hidden.'

'Ok, but what does the agreement say?'

'It says that if there is an exchange of land in Kashmir, the side losing land will get monetary compensation. From what I understand, at that time they had almost decided the boundaries.'

'I don't understand. Can you be clearer?'

'Based on the agreement, you give up your claim to all of Kashmir through which the Chinese One Belt One Road project passes. India takes it. We will nationalize everything there, including the Chinese projects. Their investment there has been over $150 billion. There will be all sorts of problems in China. You on the other hand, get to throw the Chinese out of Pakistan once and for all.'

'And lose Kashmir?!'

'Look around you, General. You've already lost all of Pakistan. Would you rather salvage that or try to hold onto a pipe dream? You will be a hero in Pakistan for throwing out the Chinese. You get to hold onto the part of Kashmir where One Belt One Road doesn't pass through. India will compensate you for land lost. USA will bail out your economy. In fact, all your debts will be forgiven—to the US, to the IMF, the ADB, and even the Saudis. All Chinese assets will be nationalized—they lose everything.'

'What about the Kashmiri people?'

'Kashmiris will have a choice. They won't automatically become Indian citizens. They can choose to remain Pakistani and continue to remain in Kashmir. We will use the formula the Chinese used when they took over Hong Kong. It will be a special zone. This will mean minimal domestic blowback for you.'

'I don't know whether it is worth it.'

'General, it is completely your decision. But if the Chinese continue to dictate terms to you—is *that* worth it?'

'And what about the Chinese?'

'This One Belt One Road is their dream project. Do you know when did the United Kingdom and France cease to be global powers? After all, they were victors of World War II and had a sizeable colonial empire even till the 1960s.'

'I think you are about to tell me.'

'The Suez Canal. All of the world's trade passed through the Suez Canal, and once UK and France lost control of the Suez Canal, they were reduced to being American lackeys. One Belt One Road is China's Suez Canal. Its existence threatens American domination of the world economy. The Americans would like nothing more than to perpetuate Pax Americana.'

'And India doesn't want a Pax Indica?'

'At the moment, we just don't want the Chinese to be the global bullies. Americans, for all their faults, are at least a few oceans away. We take away China's Suez Canal and all their partners in Asia, Africa, and the Middle East will think twice before signing up. Given that we will expose their role in the terror attacks after this, and exonerate Pakistan, not only will you look good, but the global community will put China in the dock. Their economy will take a massive hit. Americans reckon that they foresee a political purge and a major economic downturn, setting that country back by at least two decades.'

'Ok, but why now?'

'Because right now, you are recognized as the *de jure* Head of Government in Pakistan, even if Viceroy Huang and Emperor Xi are the ones who are really in charge. Earlier, some regimes still recognized Khan. If you don't do this now and the Chinese either take over or replace you with one of their own men, they will never execute that agreement.'

Chang opened his bag and removed an Amazon tablet. He connected it to the web and set the agreement in front of the General. 'We have digitized it. As soon as you sign it and hit send, the agreement will be e-mailed to the Depositary of Treaties in the office of the Secretary-General of the United Nations. You will thereby execute an agreement signed between our countries almost 30 years ago.'

'What happens then?'

'You leave the rest to us.'

Two days later

Pakistani troops entered the embassy of the People's Republic of China. Ambassador Huang and Colonel Lin were declared *persona non grata* along with all Chinese citizens currently in Pakistan and were given a 48-hour period to vacate the country.

A week later

As American troops moved in to secure the Kashmir region which Pakistan had agreed to hand over to the Indians, the Chinese troops reluctantly retreated to the Chinese border, after having defied the Pakistani diktat to withdraw their troops.

Three days later

The SSE Composite Index fell by 32 per cent at the Shanghai Stock Exchange, resulting in the single largest economic loss ever suffered in Chinese history.

Four days later

Troops of the PRC, entered the chambers of the President of the Republic and arrested him. He would face trial for crimes against the country. The new Chinese President, Zhang Lin, promised to rebuild the Chinese economy and build bridges with countries across the world. He also announced the suspension of all projects in the One Belt One Road programme of his predecessor and announced that he was under investigation for corruption as well.

A month later
Tel Aviv, Israel

Mayank approached the Indian couple sitting at one of the tables at a cafe in Tel Aviv. It was his first time in Tel Aviv and it had a distinctive European feel to it with a hint of the exotic East. *Something out of Casablanca.*

Aditi greeted him warmly. Mayank asked, 'No quip this time?'

'I am just happy to be with my husband. You haven't met Udai.' The two men shook hands.

Mayank said, 'Wow! I finally meet you. You outsmarted and outmaneuvered RAW, CIA, Pakistan, China, and God knows who else. I still can't believe you did it.'

'Yeah, I had some luck along the way.'

'Anyway, the Indian government thanks you. And we would be delighted to have you back.'

Udai shook his head. 'Not right now, but never say never.'

'So the Israelis are keeping you safe?'

Udai took a sip of his coffee. 'They have the data. They are allies of both India and the US. So they will share the data with you as they deem fit. A lot of Khan's memories were filled with anti-Israeli activities as well. They have taken down a few cells even in the last month. There are enough memories for them to make a pretty big dent into their opposition.'

'And MindCorp has offices here. You intend to rejoin?'

Udai laughed. 'Fuck that. The bastards left me out to dry. They didn't want a lawsuit, so they gave me a pretty hefty severance package. We are figuring out what to do. Maybe, we will open an Indian restaurant here. Maybe, I will take up a less stressful job. How are things back home?'

Mayank nodded. 'Sure. You can afford to take your time. There are some riots in Kashmir; some people there think that they were backstabbed by Pakistan.'

Udai asked, 'So the stone throwing has increased?'

Mayank nodded, 'Stone throwing, setting government property and buses on fire. But without Pakistani support, they won't be able to sustain any protests. Within one year, all of Kashmir will be fully integrated into the Indian Union. Something we've all been hearing since 1947, 1948. China is pretty much screwed. The Americans are in love with us. Because of the collapse of the Chinese economy, we are now officially the largest economy in Asia, and the second largest economy in the world. There is even talk of Pax Indica.'

Udai smiled. 'Best of luck to you with your plans and games of global domination.'

They shook hands. Mayank asked, 'So, will I meet you again?'

Udai looked at Aditi and shrugged. 'Never say never.'

Acknowledgements

Firstly, I would like to thank my wife, Phoram, for bearing with my idiosyncrasies and absurd schedules. I am also thankful to Mr Chinni Nihalani and his team at Promoshop India, for his inputs in the content and in marketing. Additionally, my publishers, Trisha De Niyogi and Tultul Niyogi from Niyogi Books, have been prompt and deserve kudos. My close friend from freshman year, Rohan Tejura who has always been the first one to read my work and give his honest feedback. My editor, Arunima Ghosh, has been thoroughly professional and has delivered more than I expected. Lastly, I would like to thank to my parents, for continuing to have faith in me.

Reviews of *The Tenth Unknown* by the same author

'Great idea...never read an Indian book like this...racy, well-informed...very interesting for a movie.'

—*Shyam Benegal*

'We need more stories like this—stories about Indians told by Indians.'

—*Ratna Pathak Shah*

'Very enjoyable, informative and fast-paced. Excellent read.'

—*Prahlad Kakkar*

About the Author

Jvalant Nalin Sampat is a critically acclaimed author, who at various points of his life has lived in New York, California, and Copenhagen. But he considers Bombay his home, where he resides with his wife, Phoram, and daughter, Navya. Besides writing fiction, Jvalant writes scripts for movies and TV shows. He also serves as a director in his family firm, ICL LLP. Whilst not otherwise occupied, chances are you will find him at his local club, on the tennis court.